My Story

BASIL BRUSH

With

ANDY MERRIMAN

B🌳XTREE

First published 2001 by Boxtree
an imprint of Pan Macmillan Publishers Ltd
Pan Macmillan, 20 New Wharf Road, London N1 9RR
Basingstoke and Oxford
Associated companies throughout the world
www.panmacmillan.com

ISBN 0 752 22004 7

3 5 7 9 8 6 4 2

A CIP catalogue record for this book is available from
the British Library.

Typeset by SX Composing DTP, Rayleigh, Essex
Printed and bound by
Mackays of Chatham plc, Chatham, Kent

Picture credits: All photographs of Basil Brush © 2001 Ivan Owen's
Estate and Peter Firmin under exclusve licence to Entertainment Rights plc.
Page 3: photographs of the Misters © BBC Picture Archives (Mr Howard taken
by Chris Wedgbury for the BBC, Mr Billy taken by John Green for the BBC).
Page 4: Noël Coward © Rex Features, Queen Mother © Rex Features.
Page 5: Goldie Hawn © Rex Features, Lulu © Rex Features, Basil and Maylene
© 2001 Ivan Owen's Estate and Peter Firmin under exclusive licence to
Entertainment Rights plc. Page 6: The Oscars © Steward Cook/Rex Features,
Surfing © Tom Curran/Rex Features, Muscle Beach © Clive Dixon/Rex
Features. Page 7: Las Vegas © Rex Features, Casino chips © Rex Features,
Floorshow © Rex Features.

CONTENTS

ACKNOWLEDGEMENTS

I've been lucky enough to have had a great deal of help, encouragement and support during my long show business career – not least from my family. Much gratitude and love are due therefore to my mum and dad and to my many siblings. My dad was certainly a man of litters. Ha! Ha!

I'd also like to thank the many fellow artistes I have worked with over the years – all far too humorous to mention – Peter Firmin, everyone at Entertainment Rights and, of course, Ivan Owen, who has been a dear friend and mentor.

Some writers use a 'nom de plume' – I decided against this and used a word processor instead. Ha! Ha! For those readers who think the covers of this book are too far apart, you should blame my publisher Gordon Wise and my editor, Ingrid Connell. I, however, am grateful for Ingrid's patience and good humour.

Finally, thanks to fellow scribe, Andy Merriman for his assistance when, very occasionally, words actually failed me.

Now, I must go – I feel a sequel coming on.

CHAPTER ONE
NOW AND DEN

☆ ☆ ☆

'So I went to the dentist. He said, "Say Aaah." I said, "Why?"
He said, "My dog's died." Ha! Ha!'
My First Professional Joke – Basil Brush

'My final guest tonight is something of an institution. A treasure the nation clutched to its heart some years ago and has never wanted to let go. An all-round entertainer, a singer, actor, writer, comedian. Quite simply, he is a show business legend. Ladies and gentlemen, please welcome Mr Basil Brush!'

I was waiting anxiously 'in the wings' as Michael Parkinson finished his introduction and then strode on to the studio floor to a most marvellous welcome. The audience clapped, cheered and waved and I was overcome by their warmth. It was great to be back on BBC television, especially in the company of someone I'd always considered to be the greatest ever talk-show host, Michael Parkinson. I have to say I was a bit nervous having been away from the cathode ray for a while but Mister Michael – ever the professional – made me feel relaxed immediately.

'Basil, lovely to have you here.'

'H-e-l-l-o. It's lovely to be here, Michael. An absolute treat. And, you know, I really didn't expect a chauffeur-driven car, a slap-up lunch, flowers in the dressing room. And everything went just as I expected! Ha! Ha!'

'Now, I must admit I'm slightly wary having you on the show.'

'No need for that, Michael.'

'Yes well, I had this bird on the show once who gave me a bit of a hard time.'

'You didn't have Grace Jones on your show as well, did you?'

'Not that sort of bird. I'm talking about Emu. Now, you're not going to bite me, are you?'

I raised myself to my full height of three foot six. 'I'm not a bloomin' dog, you know!'

Michael roared with laughter and the audience applauded again, having recognized one of my famous catchphrases. 'Now, Basil, you've had a very illustrious career, which we'll talk about later . . .'

'Not too much later I hope. We don't want to run out of time.'

'I expect you have a lot of stories to tell.'

'Yes, yes, yes, Michael. This business has been good to me. Lots of telly, then there's my Hollywood career . . . do you know, I found the real Hollywood when I was there. I dug beneath the tinsel.'

'And what did you find, Basil?'

'More tinsel. Ha! Ha! Oh, I've never stopped. I've

made records, done Shakespeare, I was in a long-running Broadway musical . . . I could go on . . . and on . . . and on . . .'

'Yes, I'm sure you could, Basil. And as I said we will get on to all that later.'

'And there's that little business I undertook on behalf of the British government to save the world from an evil tyrant. But then I'm not really supposed to say anything about it. Top secret.'

'That's all well and good but perhaps it can remain a secret for a little while longer.'

'Yes, it's probably for the best, Michael. I wouldn't want to get you into trouble. Now what was it you wanted to know again? Am I interrupting too much? I'm afraid it's an old habit. It used to drive some of the chaps mad – especially Mister Derek – he used to grab my—'

'Basil! Please! I really would like to ask you about your early life.'

'Of course, Michael, why didn't you say so? Well, did you know that I was born at an early age, and before I was ten I was nine. Boom! Boom!'

'Y-e-s . . . I understand you weren't always the well-behaved Basil that we know and love – especially when you were younger.'

'I'm afraid it's true – my parents couldn't wait to get rid of me. In fact, my mother used to wrap my sandwiches in road maps. There was one occasion I was so naughty – my parents left home.'

Michael rocked back in his chair and wiped a mirthful tear from his eye, 'I don't believe you. Go on, tell us about your parents.'

'My father was a bit of a rogue, but a man who would do anything to give his kids the best possible start in life. Worked day and night selling door-to-door. I suppose you could say he was the original Brush salesman. Ha! Ha! He was an enormous influence in my life, always a great support to me.

'My mother was really quite beautiful – luckily it was from her that I inherited my looks. She also inspired me to follow her into show business. She sang and played the accordion. Very successfully. She appeared in variety – 'The Virtuoso Vixen' was her billing matter. She was determined that one of her litter would make it in this profession.'

'Fascinating. And, of course, you had lots of siblings?'

'We were a lot of mouths to feed and there always seemed to be a new litter on the way. It was never easy for my mum and dad, but we always had enough food and a warm place to sleep, and we had the unconditional love of both our parents. And it wasn't just my brothers and sisters – we had a large extended family who were always around.'

Mister Michael looked intrigued. 'Go on.'

'Well, our home seemed to be open den to various members of the Brush clan – some of whom were, shall we say, of very dubious character. I had this uncle who was a bit of thief. He stole a purse but he got away with it. Told the judge he hadn't been feeling well and that he'd thought the change would do him good. He became a kleptomaniac but he's all right now – he's taking something for it. And then two of my cousins were always getting into trouble. In fact they were arrested again only the other day. One was drinking battery acid and the other was eating fireworks.

They charged one and let the other one off.'

Michael and the audience seemed to be enjoying every minute of the interview and so was I. I had been away from British television for too long.

'Anyway, those days are long gone, Michael. I'm looking forward to the future, my new sitcom, and I'm also here to plug my autobiography.'

Michael looked a bit bemused. 'Oh, um, I didn't know about that – my researchers didn't . . . I had no idea you'd written an autobiography.'

'Actually I haven't. But now that I've mentioned it, I think it's not a bad idea . . .'

And that's how it all began. Reminiscing with Michael Parkinson had actually got me thinking about my past life, and although nostalgia isn't what it used to be I decided that it was time I shared some secrets with my public. After a few cream sodas in the BBC Television Centre bar, I hurried home and began to scribble a few notes.

Despite some financial hardships, my childhood was pretty idyllic. Our home was a cosy little den underneath the roots of an oak tree at the end of a croquet lawn at the local manor house. It had originally been built by rabbits but an enterprising badger had enlarged and improved it. In years to come he was to have his own television makeover series, *Changing Dens*. With two doting parents and the fierce loyalty of all my siblings I always felt secure no matter what happened.

As I said to Michael Parkinson, my dad had a huge influence on me and being the oldest in the litter we enjoyed the sort of close relationship that fathers and first born often experience. We used to play football and hunt together and I remember our fishing trips with particular fondness. One of these expeditions was particularly significant; we were on our way down to the river bank at the bottom of the manor house when my dad asked me if I had any worms. 'Yes,' I said, 'but I'm still going fishing.' My dad laughed and looked at me proudly. 'That's not bad, son.'

When we got home he told the rest of the family about my joke. They all giggled and slapped me on the back. I hadn't thought it was that funny but it had obviously tickled them. I enjoyed the brief adulation and had only to say 'worms' to get the whole family doubled up in hilarity. I was very pleased with myself and decided I wanted more of this sort of attention. From then on it became a ritual that whenever Dad and I went fishing I would have to make him laugh. 'Hey, Dad, do you know what has sharp teeth, a tail, scales and a suitcase? Give up? A pike going on holiday!' 'Why did the salmon cross the road ? 'Cos it was tied to the chicken.' 'What did one rock pool say to the other? Show me your mussels.' 'What sits at the bottom of the sea and shivers? A nervous wreck.'

I had inadvertently conceived my first comedy routine. How wonderful it would be, I thought, to be able to create words that would make people laugh so uncontrollably that nothing else mattered. The idea excited me so much that at first I couldn't sleep for several nights. I would lie, curled amongst the soft fur of my siblings, dreaming up jokes and punch lines, whispering them to myself to perfect my phrasing and timing.

My first proper audience was, naturally enough, my unsuspecting brothers and sisters. Every Friday night after tea I would insist on them curling up at my feet whilst I rehearsed my act. I soon tried this humour lark out at school too. I was quite small for my age and to save myself from being bullied I found the best form of defence was attack. A triple pronged manoeuvre: a quick quip would distract them, a pun would leave them groaning and then I'd follow up with a belting punchline. It always worked. Anyone who upset me would feel the lash of my tongue and I was rather good at the old insults: 'You're so dim you tiptoe past the medicine cabinet so you don't wake the sleeping pills,' or 'I heard you broke your leg sweeping leaves. What did you do – fall out of the tree?' This usually deflated any trouble and at the same time would entertain my school friends.

Later, my dad furthered my fascination with the world of comedy when, somehow, he managed to procure a record player. I became completely immersed in the joys of listening to famous comedy records like Bob Newhart's *Driving Instructor*, the stories of Gerald Hoffnung and the monologues of Joyce Grenfell. As I sat for hour upon hour, utterly entranced, I realized this was how I could start to fulfil my dreams. I could write jokes and try to sell them to professional comedians. That would give me a foot in the door of show business. It was suddenly obvious, like a blinding light of revelation. If I wanted to be a comedian the way to start would be to write for other people.

In the best tradition of show business matriarchy, my mother had always hoped that, just like Minnie Marx before her, she would be able to produce (in every sense) a talented troupe of artistes. She often spoke of her dreams and aspirations for 'The Five Brushes' a knockabout comedy singing act that she had always dreamed would top the bill at the Palladium. Unfortunately for her, but fortunately for me, I was the only one who showed any interest and indeed – if you'll pardon my modesty – talent.

Having worked in variety she had remained in touch with some of her performing pals, or pros as we in the business call them, and after a few phone calls she got the address of a young magician and comedian called Tommy Cooper. My parents encouraged me to send him some material, as they called it, and so I sent him my best joke. (The one about the dentist and the dead dog.) I waited expectantly for his reply.

This exciting period coincided with another landmark in my life. It was time for me to graduate, as our American friends say, from the cosy environs of Reynard Grammar School into the big world outside. I have to say, somewhat immodestly although truthfully, that I had done rather well at school being an unusual combination of athlete and aesthete. And had it not been for my discovering the world of comedy I would certainly have attended Oxford. But everything was now up in the air and whilst waiting for my big showbiz break I needed to earn some money. Believe it or not, I actually found work at the local farm where I was employed as a sheep counter. This didn't go too well because every time I started to count them I fell asleep. Ha! Ha! The gentleman farmer was, however, very sympathetic and found me an alternative job as a sort of vulpine scarecrow. This line of work was actually much better suited to my personality and I just used to stand in the centre of a field looking as terrifying as I could. In fact, I was so good at doing this that the birds used to return the corn that they had stolen the year before!

It seemed ages but it was in fact only few weeks later when a letter arrived from Tommy Cooper saying that he was going to use my joke and asking me to send more. I was ecstatic. And I was sure that when other comedians heard the joke they would want to know who Mr Cooper's writer was and then they would all be clamouring for my services.

But although I was now a professional gag writer, I soon realized that if the comics didn't actually come knocking on my door, I would have to seek them out. The terrible truth was that if I really was to build on my initial success, I would have to drag myself away from my beloved family, friends and the manor to which I'd become accustomed.

Although we have always primarily been a country family, happiest amongst the hedgerows, copses and silage heaps of rural England, London was the capital of dreams and the place where I would have to seek my fortune, like Dick Whittington and Ken Livingstone. Between you and me, there was another temptation to lure me to the big smoke. On a day trip with my father to see the ravens at the Tower of London (he didn't manage to catch any I'm pleased to say) I made a discovery that was going to change my life. I ate my first jelly baby.

Those deliciously divine little devils immediately captured my taste buds and my heart. Those sweets proved to be an endless source of comfort to me throughout my childhood years and a passion that remains deep in my soul to this very day. In London not only was there the prospect of fame, success and a glittering show business career but very likely an endless supply of jelly babies too.

CHAPTER TWO
THE GREAT ESCAPE

'Basil is not just a natural comedian – he is also a natural born leader. It was obvious from the start that he would be the one to get us out of there. The chaps all relied on him and he didn't let anyone down. But then he never has done. We are all in his debt. I'm now going to repeat that whilst drinking a glass of water. Basil is not . . .'

Sandy Harrington, ventriloquist

'Gottle of geer.'

Percy, Sandy's dummy

After emotional farewells with family and friends, I took the coach to London and found myself walking down Russell Square on my way to the Sunnydale Hotel. A relative of mine from Huddersfield had recommended it to me. The proprietor, Linda Crabtree, a delightfully attractive woman of thirty-nine (she was apparently a great Jack Benny fan) used to feed my aunt's litter when times were hard and they had been forced to seek urban sustenance. Mrs Crabtree had since moved to London to pursue a show business career, but had had to cut down on engagements because of her ankles.

The Sunnydale Hotel was something of a theatrical experience in itself. From the moment you walked up the front steps, past the two plastic urns full of plastic geraniums, you knew you were in a home that was greatly loved. The floral theme continued once you were through the door, with endless vases and posies, swags and pot pourris of dried, plastic, silk and paper blossoms. It made me sneeze the moment I crossed the threshold, as if there was real pollen in the air rather than the clouds of swirling dust that Mrs Crabtree's feather duster disturbed afresh each morning.

Mrs Crabtree and I hit it off from the start and I soon settled into my comfortable and surprisingly spacious room. I was missing my family but this was the start of my show business adventure and I just had to grin and bear it. Every afternoon we shared a cup of tea and a home-made scone in the lounge and discussed my progress. Actually, there was very little to discuss on that front. Despite sending more gags to several comedians I still hadn't got a regular income.

I took the time to explore London. The city was even more exciting than I thought. It was the sixties and the streets were full of hippies and dropouts. People dressed any way they wanted and you didn't have to be a plumber to wear denim. Everyone was wearing jeans. Even those that shouldn't, did, and ogling onlookers would ask themselves, 'Does the end justify the jeans?'

It was the time of the mini – skirts and cars. There

were discos, jazz clubs and various nightspots offering all sorts of entertainment. I also frequented Tin Pan Alley, Charing Cross Road, where singers, songwriters and song pluggers operated. Professional rivalry was rife: I overheard one well-known vocalist say to a composer, 'That last number you wrote – I think it's such a haunting melody.' The composer replied, 'I'm not surprised – you've murdered it enough times.'

This was the ocean of show business in which I wanted to immerse myself, but at the moment I wasn't even able to dip my toe in the water. Then one day I was sitting in Eddy's bar, blowing the froth off my coffee and reading *The Stage* when I saw this advertisement: 'Versatile comic wanted to join concert party for summer season at Frinton holiday camp. No audition necessary. Must be hilarious. Write Box 345.' I sipped my frothy coffee and got a laugh from the next table for my milk moustache. I thought of it as some sort of sign. Perhaps I should have a go.

The trouble was that the summer season was still a few weeks away and even if I did get the job, goodness knows how long it would be before I got my first pay packet. I knew I was going to have to throw myself on Mrs Crabtree's mercy, or else return home with my brush between my legs.

When I went to see her, she was 'resting the feet' and listening to a recording of Russ Conway. She had a medicinal martini by her side. 'Right painful they are today. Would you mind?' Mrs Crabtree had requested a massage of her pedal extremities before and I was always happy to oblige. She plonked her ankles in my lap. 'You've got magic paws, Basil,' she would say as I set to work. I'd never considered that they were 'magic' and I was sure that she was going over the top but . . . it certainly gave me paws for thought.

'Would you like a drink, yourself, Basil?'

'No thanks, I'm fine.'

'You know,' Mrs Crabtree said, looking wistful, 'I used to drink absinthe, in my younger days. It was lovely, but it did make me feel sentimental.'

'Ah well,' I said, 'absinthe does make the heart grow fonder. Ha! Ha!'

Mrs Crabtree giggled, 'And now look at me, I'm just an incurable rheumatic.'

'Oh how the malady lingers on!'

Several puns later we were helpless with laughter. I thought this was a good time to broach the awkward question of rent. 'I have a bit of a problem,' I confessed. She patted the arm of her chair, inviting me to sit close to her and tell her all about it. I explained about the temporary cash flow inadequacy and promised I would take the first job I was offered in order to make up the arrears I would owe her if she allowed me to stay on. She reacted differently to the way I had expected. She told me not to worry for a moment, she trusted me completely and began tweaking the collar of my shirt. She leaned closer and I could smell a pitted olive on her breath.

'I have an idea how you could pay for your board and lodging.'

'Oh yes,' I answered nervously.

'What do you think?' she asked, tickling me pleasantly under the chin.

'I'd be very happy to do whatever was useful,' I said doubtfully.

A cheerful smile creased her lips. 'Come with me, then,' she said, taking her glass in one hand and leading me from her private quarters with the other. She took me into the room that she wistfully referred to as 'the residents' lounge bar'. It was a small room, filled with wooden-armed chairs upholstered in green imitation leather. In the corner was a heavily mirrored bar, complete with rows of upside down bottles, a few upturned Babycham glasses, and a jar of Maraschino cherries. She lifted me on to the slippery surface of the bar and gestured round at the room.

'What do you think?' she asked again.

'Very nice,' I said, rather at a loss. 'Very cosy. Very homely.'

'We'll call it the cabaret room from now on. Three shows a day, breakfast, tea time and after dinner.'

'Pardon?'

'This will be your stage.' She slapped the highly polished Formica bar top affectionately. 'It'll give you a chance to practise your craft in front of a live audience, and it'll help me to keep the punters on the premises, drinking and spending money. This room will go down in history as the place you launched your career. We'll be able to put up a plaque outside once you're famous. Tourists will flock here from all over the world . . .'

I could see she was spinning away from reality at a frightening speed, but I could also see that this was indeed a chance for me. I would be able to practise my craft in front of a live audience. If I could make travelling salesmen and retired gentlewomen on budget shopping expeditions laugh at breakfast time I could do anything. It would also mean I had a roof over my head and three square meals a day.

14

'Okay,' I said. 'It's a deal.'

And so I opened in my first solo show, and what a baptism of fire it was. Often my audiences could be counted on one paw, and they might well be the same person as the previous four or five shows, which meant I could never reuse the same material. Each performance had to be fresh, sharp and topical. It was the birth of modern satire, similar to the sort of thing Peter Cook and his friends were working on in other parts of the city. This was a London crowd, used to sophisticated entertainment and quite different to my first audience of adoring siblings in the cosy confines of the family den. I would be up half the night writing new material and trying it out on the mirror above the basin, which I could only reach if I balanced one foot on each of the dripping taps. It was a tremendous self-discipline and I don't believe any comedian can say he's truly learned his business until he's done a season in bed and breakfast, three shows a day, competing with the background noise of Mrs Crabtree's Hoover and the smell of Izal and home cooked fry-ups.

I was hoping that before long a big time promoter or booking agent would pass through the Sunnydale Hotel, perhaps over-nighting after a late flight into Heathrow, and would catch the act. I was confident that if I could just get seen, it was only a matter of time before I was discovered.

The Sunnydale might not have been the London Palladium or *Opportunity Knocks*, but it was still a showcase for my talent. Mrs Crabtree arranged a series of publicity photos for me and attached the most flattering one to the front door. Underneath she pinned a large notice advertising the show and suggesting non-residents should rush to see it before it transferred to the West End and ticket prices went through the roof. I have to admit it gave me a flutter of excitement to see that poster every time I went up or down the front steps, which I did quite a bit on the first day she put it up.

I had now sorted out my accommodation and work but my personal life was a bit bereft. I didn't really know anyone and I realized that however much I was enjoying the bright lights and glamorous London lifestyle, I was missing the country. No matter how hard I tried I just could not get used to the sound of birds coughing. The pain at times was unbearable. I had to get help.

Mrs Crabtree had seen all this before with other residents and suggested I join 'Bucolics Anonymous' – a self-help group for all of us in the same position. Every week a group of rustic rejects would meet on Hampstead Heath (it was the closest we could get to the countryside) and swap experiences. These regular meetings were a constant source of inspiration and support and helped me immeasurably during those difficult times. To be able to meet with other exiled countryphiles who were all in the same situation was the best assistance anyone could get. Although I cannot name names there was Percy Thrower, Fred Hargreaves, the panel of *Gardeners' Question Time* and some of *The Archers* cast, most of whom remain friends to this day.

It seemed, however, that I was destined to return to the countryside – albeit briefly – when I received notification that I had been successful in my application for the 'Frinton Frolics'. I was expected in Essex the following week.

Mrs Crabtree was of course disappointed that I had to end our cabaret agreement but, being an old trooper, she understood. She also promised to find me a room at the Sunnydale on my return. I cheekily asked if I could have a room that looked out on the garden. 'I think you'd be better off with a room that overlooks the rent,' she quipped. What a wonderful woman!

I'd never been to Frinton although I'd heard quite a lot about the resort. It was situated on the east coast – except when the tide came in, and then it was on the west coast. Ha! Ha! And in spite of a fresh east wind, Frinton was rather stuffy. No pubs, no ice cream vendors. No hamburgers or fish and chips. Nevertheless it made me realize that entertainment within the camp would be a must for the holidaymakers and what's more I would have a captive audience. Little did I know then just how true that would be.

Now I don't know whether my fame had preceded my arrival but I had a police escort all the way from Frinton railway station to the holiday camp. And flattered though I was, I did feel a bit of a fool running along between four motorcycles. Ha! Ha! This was actually nothing in comparison with what was to follow. There was still a light dusting of snow on the ground, despite the fact that the Frinton Fun Camp was preparing for its summer season. The redcoated guards on the gate were stamping their feet and blowing into their hands with steamy breath. They fingered their walkie-talkies threateningly, their eyes hidden behind dark sunglasses, despite the gloom that surrounded the bright searchlights mounted on either side of the gate. The fencing was high around the perimeter of the camp, topped with twists of barbed wire. The frosted countryside lay silent and deserted all around.

While I stood shivering, the guards searched my small suitcase for any forbidden items. Apparently they didn't want to encourage pilfering amongst the guests and so any possessions beyond those directly required for personal hygiene and previously specified medical conditions were to be confiscated, listed and returned upon release from the contract. In a fit of extravagance I'd purchased a small bag of jelly babies at the station kiosk in London. I'd eaten most of them on the train but had been saving the last few in case I was too late for supper and needed a snack after lights out.

One of the redcoats lifted the crumpled paper bag out of my suitcase between a distasteful finger and thumb. The tension could have been cut with a knife. I didn't want to lose the jelly babies. I struck a deal, my well-practised bonhomie by now becoming a little forced, and we split the babies between us. The barriers lifted and they nodded me through. I was on the inside at last.

'Follow me,' said a lantern-jawed redcoat as he led me to my chalet. Quite a pretty Swiss type hut with window boxes that looked as if some extensive conversion had taken place. The sign on the door, 'P.O.W.', was a bit disconcerting, but the guard put me at ease by kindly explaining that the Prince of Wales had stayed there. As he showed me the interior, he pointed to some clothes on the back of the door. 'That's your uniform. I suggest you put it on straightaway so that we can recognize you instantly.' He pointed to a white shirt, flannels, garish striped tie and an emerald green blazer.

'I'm afraid green's not really my colour, you see with my reddish—'

'Too bad. The so-called entertainers wear green jackets, we wear red jackets and Colonel Trautmann – you haven't met him yet – always wears grey.'

'I see we're colour coded. I hope we don't clash.'

'Oh, no. There are no clashes here. We are all one big happy family. Colonel Trautmann says so.' With a sinister smile, he left. To my surprise, he locked the door behind him. There was something fishy going on . . . and I didn't like the stench.

The following day I was ordered to report to the concert hall. That's a laugh. Concert hall. A gymnasium with foldaway chairs, more like. The posters outside read, 'Frinton Frolics – an evening of mirth, music and magic. Complete change of programme every two weeks.' Hello, I thought, that means two different routines and that wasn't even in the small print. At least I was able to meet my fellow entertainers. First to introduce themselves were ventriloquist Sandy Harrington and his dummy, Percy. They looked extraordinarily alike and so I made a mental note that it was Percy who had the rosy cheeks. Next to offer the firm handshake was 'Ginger' Johnson's One Man Band – 'only myself to blame' – followed by Fay Francis, the vocalist with an unusual range (the one where the deer and the antelope play), 'Merlin', The Magical Marvel – aka Uncle Chuckles, available for children's parties – and the knockabout comedy act, Novak and Good. Yours truly was billed as 'Principal comic'.

Well, here we were. Seven of us. Although I wasn't sure about the 'Magnificent' bit yet.

It was time to meet the entertainments manager,

Colonel Trautmann. A tall wiry man with a pronounced stoop – which he pronounced 'stoop' – he bore a remarkable resemblance to the actor Anton Diffring. He ordered us to sit and climbed the stairs on to the flimsy stage which was to serve as a showcase for my talents throughout that summer. He appeared not to notice the cold winds that were whistling through the gaps in the wooden walls, making the teeth of his audience chatter in a sort of choral Morse code.

'Welcome to the "Frinton Frolics". I am Max Trautmann and I have been here since 1942. I love it as you will grow to love it. And,' he paused for dramatic effect, 'you *will* grow to love it. You see, I was a prisoner of war in this camp. At the end of the hostilities, I decided to stay on in England and your very helpful War Office let me rent the building and grounds. As you can see, very little has changed but this is how I like it.' I could see that the Colonel was actually moved to tears as he described how he'd first fallen in love with the place when he'd been behind bars here during the war.

At the end of his lecture – no questions were allowed – we were dismissed. Tomorrow rehearsals would begin in earnest. From then on we didn't have a moment to ourselves. We worked hard and for the following few weeks underwent gruelling rehearsals under the watchful eye of Max Trautmann who I think had seen *Sunset Boulevard* too many times, because by now he had added a riding crop and leather breeches to his steel grey jacket.

Conditions in the camp were terrible. The food was inedible and came in such small portions we were constantly hungry. The redcoats were quite nasty and particularly mean to us greencoats. There was a rumour that they had once been entertainers but had failed miserably and were now forced to wear the hated red uniforms. I also couldn't get used to the fact that they searched our rooms every night and dragged us out of bed every morning at five o'clock for 'roll call'. Early mornings have never been my best time of day and the others used to refer to me as 'the crank of dawn'.

When the holidaymakers finally arrived, the redcoats were in their element, bullying, teasing and mistreating the poor guests who were actually paying for the privilege of this happy holiday. Of course, being true professionals, we gave our all in the true showbiz style. I think the guests were grateful for the laughter and musicality, not to mention the warmth (the only heat in the freezing camp) that our performances generated.

One night I saw a couple of holidaymakers being dragged back over the perimeter by a couple of redcoats, or goons as we now called them (I was against this as I had always been a fan of the show), whilst attempting a break out. I heard their strained cries for help and their feeble protests: 'I can't take it any more, please let me go. I'll even go to Minehead.' I realized that I felt exactly the same – although not about Minehead – and that I too had to get away from this dismal place.

The following night, whilst enjoying our ritual cup of cocoa backstage at the theatre, I thought I'd judge the mood of the concert party. I noticed that Ginger Johnson was looking at pictures of two women somewhat wistfully.

'Girlfriends, Ginger?'

'Yes, Basil.'

'Pretty girls. Missing them?'

'God, yes. Both of them. Kate is the sweetest, most

loyal girl a chap could have and Edith – well she's just a whirlwind . . . enchanting. You never know what to expect.'

'Tough business. Not really fair to keep them both hanging on.'

'I know, Basil, but I like them both equally.'

'Ginger, you must face up to a decision. You must make your choice – you can't have your Kate and Edith too.'

Ginger avoided my stare and tried to gaze through the bars of the window. 'Do you realize it will still be summer at home. The incandescent petunias will be blooming, the fuchsia and the hydrangeas will be heavy with flowers and the air will be filled with magic perfumes.'

'Where do you live, Ginger?'

'Wapping.'

I approached George Good, half of the comedy act. The funny one.

'How are you settling in here?'

'Fairly well, Basil, but there's one thing I miss terribly. And that's cricket.'

I noticed that a tear was forming in George's eye. 'Are you all right, old man?'

'It's nothing . . . I don't usually get emotional . . . it's just that it's been so long since I've seen a game. Ah, how it all comes back, the excitement of the scrum, the lineouts, the thrill of a touchdown.'

I paused. 'It has been a long time, hasn't it? I hardly like to mention this, George, but that's rugger.'

George looked horrified and covered his head in his hands. I realized that his mind was going. He had spent too much time in the cooler. I had seen quite enough and decided to call the greencoats together. 'Gather around, chaps. I hope you don't mind my referring to you as a chap, Fay, but it will be a lot easier – especially if I ever write my autobiography. Merlin, please put away that mouth organ, it's not in your act and it's been done to death. Now, look here, it's time for action. Our careers are going nowhere here and neither are we.'

I told them that I wasn't prepared to see out my contract and planned to escape before the end of our engagement. It transpired that they all felt exactly the same as I did, but to keep morale high had opted not to say a word.

Sandy interjected, 'What about the holidaymakers – are we going to leave them here?'

'No,' I was quick to answer, 'they're our audience and they've suffered enough. If we look after the public – the public will look after us. They must go free.' I had already conceived a plan for their escape but didn't want to make it public just yet.

Within a few hours we had formed an escape committee and the entertainers soon agreed that, with my natural leadership skills and my previous experience as a cub, I was the chap to take charge. Within a week, a number of cunning schemes were already in operation and another meeting was called to discuss progress. Fay Francis was posted as a guard. Everyone was present apart from Merlin who was trying out a new levitation trick.

I started the ball rolling, 'Righto, chaps, where have we got to?'

Novak and Good were very proud of themselves. 'We've already dug ten tunnels; we started with Tom, Dick and Harry then we added Abbot and Costello, Laurel and Hardy and Groucho, Harpo and Chico.'

'Well that's what I call variety,' I joked.

'Yeah, except the redcoats discovered them.'

Ginger Johnson was next. 'I'm willing to sacrifice my freedom for the rest of you. I could create a diversion whilst you escape. I'll play my rendition of "Alexander's Ragtime Band" and make a lot of noise with my drum kit.'

I shook my head. 'I'm afraid it will never work. You never think things through, Ginger, that's your trouble. You're too cymbal minded.' I turned to the ventriloquist, 'And as for you, Sandy, what happened to your foolproof plan?'

'The plan was sound enough, sir, but somehow the chaps got left behind and three of my dummies escaped.'

'And what on earth are all these empty corned beef tins for?'

'I'm going to build an aeroplane, sir.'

'Your plans are far too ambitious, Sandy. We cannot sustain these daredevil attempts. The redcoats aren't fools you know. If this sort of thing goes on, we will have our privileges removed.'

'That could be rather painful, sir.'

I ignored this appallingly obvious remark but made a mental note to put it in my act at a later date. 'Listen to me, the redcoats seem to know of our schemes in advance. If you ask me there's an informer amongst us.'

As soon as the gasp of horror had subsided, Ginger was quick to add, 'I think you're right, sir, and I've got a suspicion that it's Merlin, The Magical Marvel.'

'What makes you think that?'

'He hangs around with Colonel Trautmann an awful lot and there's something rather un-British about him. Have you ever seen him drinking tea?'

'No, why?'

'Well, sir . . . he doesn't crook his little finger. Look, through the window. There he is now, standing in the flower bed.'

'It's possible the redcoats could have planted him,' I agreed, and acted quickly. 'Get him in here. We'll soon see if he's Trautmann's stooge.' George Good went outside to fetch the confederate conjuror whilst Ginger volunteered to do the dirty work: 'Leave this to me, sir. I'll soon put Merlin to the test.'

'Remember, Ginger, this calls for a cunning and subtle approach.'

'Of course, sir.'

Merlin entered nervously, 'You wanted to see me, sir?'

'Ah, yes, come in. Ginger wants a word with you.'

'Hello, Merlin, we were just going to have some grub. Care to join us?'

'Thank you.'

'Which would you prefer – crumpets or sauerkraut?'

'Oh, crumpets every time.'

Ginger turned to me and shrugged his shoulders, 'Well, he seems sound enough to me, sir.'

I needed to be absolutely sure that Merlin wasn't a redcoat in disguise and so I asked him, 'How do you get an elephant out of the theatre?'

He replied as quick as a flash, in true showbiz style, 'You don't – it's in his blood.'

I was delighted and relieved. 'Good man, Merlin, I was testing you and you've come through with flying colours. You're a true greencoat.'

At that moment, Fay burst into her own inimitable rendition of 'On a wonderful day like today' – a prearranged signal that Max Trautmann was on his way. We moved the stove, hid the wooden horse and drove away the motor bike just in time before the Colonel entered.

'Ah, so there you are, Herr Brush – oh, I think that deserves a Boom! Boom!, does it not?'

'What is it you want, Trautmann?'

'Brush, unless you want to suffer serious consequences, these ridiculous plans to escape have got to stop. Your attempts are futile. Did you really think we are so stupid we would fail to notice two thousand holidaymakers floating skywards in a home made balloon?'

'You swine. What happened to them?'

'What do you think? They escaped.'

We all cheered and punched the air in excitement. Our public was safe.

The Colonel continued, 'I will find out who is responsible for organizing these escape plans. There will be a full-scale interrogation and, if necessary, wholesale punishment.'

'Just a minute!' I was outraged. 'You must understand, it is the duty of every true British entertainer to try and escape from an unfair contract. It's in the Cromer Convention. Signed at the end of the pier, 1948.'

'I care nothing for conventions and your pier is nothing to write home about either.' With that Trautmann stormed out.

'Now what are we going to do?' Fay Francis was close to tears.

I remained as calm and unflappable as ever. 'Don't worry – he won't be bothering us again. I've secreted a rocket in the shaft of his shooting stick; it's due to go off at dawn.'

Fay said breathlessly, 'Does that mean . . . ?'

'Yes – he won't be down for breakfast. Right, it's time for us to leave. I've kept a little secret from all of you – I hope you don't mind. You see, for the last week I've been burrowing, singlepawed. I finished the tunnel an hour ago. We get into it under the stage trapdoor . . .'

Clutching our few belongings and props we made our way quietly and for the very last time to the concert hall. We hugged, wished each other luck and then, one by one, dropped into the darkness.

We surfaced just outside Clacton – I had rather misjudged the length of the tunnel but at least we were free. We thought it would be safer if we split up but agreed to meet up outside the Palladium one day. We said our goodbyes and promised to write – even if it was only a musical. I also made a vow to the chaps that when all this was over and our story could be told, I would get Alec Guinness to play me. I waved goodbye until the last member of the concert party was out of sight and then went on my way. London beckoned me and, running swiftly across the Essex fields, I headed for home.

CHAPTER THREE

A BRUSH WITH FAME

'When I saw Basil at the Old Vic, I knew he was something special – his lyricism, his timing, his tenderness and his mere presence would enhance any production. Although he is without doubt one of show business's most charismatic entertainers, television's gain has been the theatre's loss. I still believe he would have been the most marvellous Falstaff – perhaps the greatest ever.'

Sir Peter Nunn-Brook
Director, National Shakespeare Company

I had gladly settled myself back into the Sunnydale Hotel and my thrice daily cabaret spot when Linda (Mrs Crabtree and I were on first name terms now) suggested that I should get myself a theatrical agent. She had someone in mind and although she was slightly disparaging about the fact that he was 'a Lanc', she seemed to think that Harry Burns of Interplanetary Entertainments would further my career much quicker than I could manage on my own.

I was picturing Harry Burns at the centre of a worldwide business empire, so the office block in Shepherd's Bush wasn't quite what I was expecting. The bare stone staircase smelled of disinfectant and the old lift shaft made alarming clanging noises. I found Mr Burns in a small back office, not the luxury suite I'd imagined being led into. He didn't even seem to have a secretary, just a telephone, an electric kettle and a toaster. The air was thick with cigar smoke, making my eyes water.

On the walls around his desk were a number of pictures of big stars – James Dean, Marlon Brando, Humphrey Bogart, that sort of thing – which looked as if they might have been cut out of magazines. There were also some signed pictures of people I didn't know, most of them women and most of them not wearing very many clothes, although one of them had managed to drape a large snake pretty imaginatively about herself.

The man himself was aged about forty and was dressed in a gold-buttoned, navy blue yachting blazer, pink shirt and silk cravat and, although the cricket season was now over, seemed to be sporting white flannels. His hair was dyed a rather jolly bright yellow and he had a large cigar between his chubby fingers which he jammed into his mouth from time to time, causing him to wheeze and let out the occasional ear splitting cough. He was just finishing a telephone call whilst he beckoned me to sit down.

'Yes, well, I'm sorry, Mike, you'll just have to go to Southsea. Let me know how it goes.' He slammed the phone down with a flourish and by way of explanation said, 'Human cannonball act – trouble is, he doesn't like to travel.'

I smiled, thinking I might be able to use that line one day.

'Hello, Basil, I would introduce myself but I already know who I am! Have a seat.' Mr Burns' accent was pure Bolton.

'Good morning, it's very good of you to see me so soon.'

'My pleasure. Now I've looked at your curriculum vitae. Sunnydale Cabaret Lounge, Frinton holiday camp. Not done much so far, have you?'

'There is the Tommy Cooper joke.'

'True, that's a start. But you do realize you'll have to write some more, don't you? I've already got one comic who's just celebrated the thirtieth anniversary of his joke.'

'Oh, I've got quite few jokes in my repertoire now,' I replied triumphantly.

'What about a comedy prop? Or an instrument? Can you play the tuba? They can be very comical.'

'No, I don't play the tuba. Sorry, Mr Burns.'

'Never apologise or explain, sunshine. It's a sign of weakness. I never do. And here's something else to take in. As far as I'm concerned, all my acts are great. Well, actually, some of them are terrible – but to me they're all great. With me, you get complete faith, loyalty and respect all at a small percentage of your fee.' Mr Burns didn't stop to draw breath, 'As we say here at Interplanetary Entertainments, "We make a world of difference to your earnings." Trust – that's the key word. Don't fret if you don't hear from me or see me for weeks on end. I'll be out there somewhere ducking and diving on your behalf. Now, do you sing?'

'A little,' I replied. 'And I could be trained.'

'Oh no,' he shook his head, as if despairing. 'We're not talking opera here.'

'Oh that's a shame, I like opera.'

'Really?' Mr Burns looked surprised. 'I've never gone for it myself. I can never understand why, when the bloke gets stabbed, instead of bleeding he sings. Do you mean, you honestly know about the *Marriage of Figaro* and *Madame Butterfly*?'

'Well not entirely. I didn't even know they were engaged. Ha! Ha! Actually, what I was hoping, Mr Burns,' I said, 'was that I could concentrate on the comedy. Writing and performing.'

Mr Burns put his cigar down rather too close to a pile of yellowing papers on his desk and adopted a serious pose. 'Let me give you a tip about comedy. The first rule is never to perform in towns where they still point at aeroplanes. That's advice you can't buy.' He retrieved his cigar and looked pleased with himself. I had no idea what he meant but I nodded sagely.

'Okay.' He sat back in his chair and put his feet up on the desk. 'Let's see the act.'

Well, of course, I had prepared a routine of the best material I had written and performed at various venues thus far. I started somewhat nervously whilst Mr Burns watched me, smiling encouragingly and making notes.

'A trout stopped a herring in the stream one day and asked, "Where's your brother?" For some reason the herring was really cross and turned on the trout angrily. "Why are you asking me? Am I my brother's kipper?"

'Actually one of my own brothers is always flying off the handle – I think he must have a screw loose . . .'

I kept it up for what seemed like an hour but was actually just over five minutes according to the Mickey Mouse clock on the wall. At one stage, chuckling loudly, Mr Burns dropped a huge pile of ash on the carpet and I remarked that *I* was the one who should be setting the place alight. Not bad for an ad-lib, I thought. Finally, he stopped me and applauded – a sort of sitting ovation. 'Excellent, Basil. You've got some great gags there and I like the "Boom! Boom!", you should work on that, build the act around it.'

Mr Burns seemed genuinely pleased and I asked him if he would consider representing me. 'It's a deal,' he said offering me his hand. 'I think we'll be good for each other.' I was delighted and held out my paw.

'Now, pin your ears back, lad. I'm going to give you some priceless advice about this world of entertainment. Show business is like a pomegranate. You have to work out which is the fruit and which are the pips and act accordingly. Eat and spit at the right time. What I'm really saying is, let the fruit be your guide.'

We then spent a few minutes discussing financial arrangements and I signed a contract – 'a formality' – which Mr Burns said he asked all his artistes to complete. As he said, quoting the words of the legendary Hollywood mogul Sam Goldwyn, 'A verbal contract's not worth the paper it's written on.'

He then took me by the arm and led me to a full-length mirror in the corner of his office. 'Right, now, the last thing is to get you some togs sorted out. Remember, at all times you must be a star. Never chance down your back passage to empty the rubbish unless you are dressed to kill. Those slacks and that sweater will never do,' he said, staring at them a little harder. 'I know exactly what we'll do. We'll go for the tweedy look – the whole Terry-Thomas, Leslie Phillips thing. Yes, that'll work. Perhaps we could call you Lord Basil,' Harry continued. 'Tell you what, I'll introduce you to my tailor. Get you sorted out with a few outfits.'

'I'm not sure how far my money will stretch,' I said doubtfully.

'Oh, don't worry about that,' he chuckled. 'Call it a generous gift. I'll deduct it from your first fee. When you're a huge star I'll be able to say I dressed you.'

'Oh, well, if you're sure?' I was overwhelmed and deeply touched. I had a patron, just like Michelangelo, my very own Medici in flannels. It seemed that everything was coming together. I was on my way.

Harry made a call and arranged for me to see his tailor immediately. The tailor turned out to be Huntsman in Savile Row. It was just as well he was paying, because I couldn't have afforded a pair of socks in a place that grand. Harry had rung ahead and told them exactly what I needed, which was also just as well because I didn't have a clue.

The tailors, elderly men in half-moon spectacles, measured and pinned and enquired about my preferences vis-à-vis pockets and pleats and vents and turn ups. I just kept saying, 'oh, you know, the usual thing,' as if I was the sort of chap who was always having clothes made for him in a place that posh. I thought I'd try and entertain them.

'Do you know I donated one trouser leg to my local

library? They said it would be a turn up for the books.'
Remembering Harry's words I added a 'Boom! Boom!'
But it didn't seem to amuse them. I also told them that I
must have a rough Scottish tweed because, 'it's the coarse
material that gets the laughs.' That didn't raise even a
smile. It was altogether a very sombre atmosphere – a bit
like playing a mid-week, winter matinee at Eastbourne.

By the time I left Savile Row, I was already equipped
with my first suit and overcoat. The rest was due to be
finished the following week. I felt like a million dollars. I
knew I had clothes that would last me a lifetime. I travelled
home, delighted with myself. I had representation with an
agent who had kindly agreed to let me keep 70 per cent of
my earnings. Mr Burns seemed to know the business
inside out and my positive feelings about him were
confirmed only a week later when I received a call from
him on the payphone at the Sunnydale Hotel. 'Listen to
this, Basil, I've got something really exciting for you. Have
you heard of the Windmill?'

'Well, we had one in our village. Some of our cousins
lived beneath it,' I replied innocently.

'No, *the* Windmill. It's a theatre. In Soho.'

'You've got me some theatre work. How marvellous.
Of course I've never really done legitimate theatre but I'm
always—'

Harry interrupted, 'Willing to learn. That's what I like
about you, Basil. Anyway, it's a fabulous job. I've got you
a six week engagement.'

Mr Burns went on to give me more details, but he
started to mumble and I couldn't exactly hear what he was
saying. I did catch something about 'waiting in the wings'.
I knew that was the title of a play by Noël Coward about

retired theatricals and although they would obviously have to slap on lots of make-up to make me look older, I was thrilled at the prospect of being in one of Mr Coward's productions.

'I'll have to give my notice in at the Sunnydale.'

'Don't you worry. There'll be no more Sunnydale Hotels for you, my son. Next stop the London Palladium.'

When I was to later break the news to Linda Crabtree, she wept from a mixture of joy for me at getting a break and sadness at losing – this time permanently – 'the best cabaret act the Sunnydale has ever seen.' But, in her own inimitable style, and showing the true grit of the Yorkshirewoman that she was, added her own favourite catchphrase, 'But you've got to do it, haven't you?' I told her I'd never forget the fact that she had given me my first break in the business, and once I was famous I'd mention her in my autobiography.

So, here goes . . . 'H-e-l-l-o, Linda!'

When I arrived at the Windmill the following day, a charming young lady led me through labyrinthine corridors past rehearsal rooms and workshops where the theatrical sets were being designed and put together. I could hear music reverberating everywhere throughout the building. I hadn't realized that *Waiting In The Wings* was a musical and I was glad that I had a reasonably decent voice. I was somewhat surprised that they had started to rehearse without me but I was also flattered that they thought I could fit in to the cast straightaway. The young lady, Desirée by name, led me backstage to the deserted dressing rooms.

'Is Mr Coward here yet?' I asked. 'Noël Coward,' I added when Desirée looked blank.

'No, I don't think so. I'm not sure that it's his sort of thing. Here, take these.'

Desirée flung me half a dozen dressing gowns and beckoned me to follow her to the side of the stage. 'When the girls come off, just make sure they each get a gown. See you later.'

Well, you can imagine my shock when I looked at the stage and saw a whole troupe of nearly naked women. They were as still as statues – not even speaking. Noël Coward's going to go mad when they see what they've done to his play, I thought. I also couldn't understand why a theatre in London's West End couldn't afford decent costumes – well, any costumes – for the actresses.

Within a couple of minutes, the curtain came down to a smattering of applause and the girls all collected their dressing gowns which I was still holding. They were terribly grateful for my help and didn't seem at all embarrassed at my presence. Of course I was to learn later that this was actually going to be my job for the next six weeks – I had completely misunderstood Mr Burns' description of my first theatrical engagement. Although the girls were very attractive in their own way, you can imagine that the job proved particularly tedious after a while and I felt that my comic skills were going to waste.

I shouldn't have worried because this was all going to change. One afternoon I was in the wings as usual, dressing gowns stacked at the ready, when the charming owner and director of the Windmill, Sheila van Damm, approached me. 'Basil, we're in trouble. We've just had a telephone call from Jimmy Edwards. He's indisposed – some sort of accident with his tuba. He's due to go on now. Can you do twenty minutes for us?'

My whole life flashed before me and nearly all of my jokes. 'Of course I can. Just give me a thirty seconds to prepare.' And that was it. I strode on stage dizzy, terrified but exhilarated and did my entire act.

I would love to say that I brought the house down but I have to say that I got a better reception at the Sunnydale. The audience was comprised of about twenty middle-aged men – all of whom seemed to be wearing raincoats although it was a lovely hot afternoon. They just didn't seem to be interested in my act. In fact I'm not sure why they were there, although they did seem to perk up when some of the girls came on to appear in another historical 'tableau vivant'.

But the lack of response from the audience didn't dispel Miss van Damm's enthusiasm. She told me I was 'terrific' and that she would find me a regular spot during the show. Of course, I later discovered that even some of the best known comics such as Stanley Holloway, Tony Hancock and Peter Sellers had all struggled at the Windmill in their early days until they found their rightful audience.

Miss van Damm kept her promise and before long I was doing several performances a day and my confidence and reputation were growing with every show. I soon realized that the punters were coming to see me and not just the girls. I loved everything about being on stage. I loved the warmth of the spotlight, the smell of the greasepaint. I loved the surge of adrenaline just before running out on stage, with its wave of accompanying nausea and the sudden urge to lock myself in a bathroom and never come out. Most of all I was addicted to the laughter and the applause.

Oh, and just in case you were worrying about some of the Windmill girls getting a bit chilly after their performances with no one to hand over the dressing gowns, you've no need to concern yourselves. I was replaced by an up-and-coming comedian by the name of . . . Benny Hill.

Now that I had a regular income and was unable to fulfil any contractual obligations at the Sunnydale, I felt it was time to move on. A couple of cousins of mine – brothers and aspiring actors Edward and James Fox – had a spare room in their Bloomsbury 'pad' and suggested that I move in with them. I was thrilled and was soon having a marvellous time with them and their friends who were studying at R.A.D.A. (yes, the Reynard Academy of Dramatic Art).

I learned an awful lot about the theatre from Edward and James and their friends and it was through them that I discovered my love of Shakespeare – I read his plays with great enthusiasm. You could say there were no holds Bard. Ha! Ha! I was also given some useful hints should I ever want to pursue a career as a serious Shakespearean actor: don't play a king because you never get a chance to sit down; if offered the role of Hamlet, turn it down and suggest that the part of Osric, a courtier, is more suited to your talents. In this way, according to the Misters Fox, there's not nearly so much to learn and you get to spend a lot more time in the pub before the final curtain call.

Not many people know this, but I was actually given the opportunity to appear for one night at the Old Vic. An actor pal, Ralph, wanted the night off and asked me to fill in for him, playing a spear-carrier in a production of *The Comedy of Errors*. I told him that I didn't know one end of a spear from another, but he explained this was just an acting term. He talked me through the part which was that of a gaoler. He advised me about breath control, the timing of the line, the pacing of delivery, the musicality of the phrasing. He reminded me that Shakespeare's text is full of sound, fury, humour and philosophy. If only I'd had a speaking part! Still, he also warned me not to bump into the furniture, wipe my nose or check my flies. And, as I was playing the gaoler not to forget to do some 'business' with the keys.

Anyway, I have to say it all went very well and I was considered to be a great success. At least, I seemed to stop the audience from coughing whilst I was on stage which in some circles is considered a glittering performance. I was hooked, but unfortunately this was my only appearance at the Old Vic to date. It was a hugely enjoyable time for me and I still refer to it as the 'Dawn of a New Error'.

My engagement at the Windmill was just coming to an end when I got another call from Harry Burns. I had been warned by new-found friends at R.A.D.A that agents were egotistical, often behaved like cattle and were only in it for the money. But Harry was different, this was my second call in a couple of months and with it came more work.

'A mate of mine at Rediffusion is casting a children's telly series,' he announced.

'Television!' I was excited.

'Well, I told you it was only a matter of time, Basil.'

'This is stupendous news, Mr Burns. But am I ready for television?'

'And I would answer that by saying is television ready for you, Basil?' he laughed triumphantly. 'Of course you're ready. Primed to perfection!

'They're expecting you down there at three this afternoon, looking smart.' Harry continued. 'Now I've spent a lot of time and energy getting you this show, so I'm going to waive my usual fee and take 75 per cent instead. Don't be late.'

This seemed an awful lot of money, but still, a telly job! It was all very exciting. My career seemed to be going better and better. I couldn't wait to tell my family.

When I arrived at the address I'd been given, an echoing church hall somewhere off Baker Street, I was surprised to find a queue of people stretching around the block. I strolled to the front and found a girl with a clipboard who seemed to be in charge of keeping everyone back from the door.

'I'm Basil Brush,' I told her, and mentioned Harry Burns. 'Fill this in and go to the back of the queue,' she said, looking harassed and thrusting a form into my hand.

I made my way back along the line of circus acts and variety turns, many of them tuning up their voices, testing their jokes or exercising their ballet muscles up against the graffiti-covered walls of the hall.

I had just started to complete the application form when I was interrupted by a gruff voice: 'Hullo there, I'm Spike McPike. Children's entertainer. I'm the token Scotsman.'

The speaker was a rather dour looking hedgehog who was standing in the queue just ahead of me, clutching his own application form and a small hip flask, which he proffered to me.

'Would you like a nip?'

'No thank you,' I said, 'it's a little early for me – unless it's cream soda.'

Mr McPike looked at me pityingly. 'If I'd known you were coming I'd have brought you some dandelion and burdock.' He took a quick swig. 'You'll have to excuse me, but I've done rather a lot of these auditions and I'm suffering from a bit of bottle fatigue.'

'Don't you mean battle fatigue?' I asked.

'I know what I mean.' Mr McPike took a final swallow from his hip flask before returning it to his pocket.

'Brush,' I said, shaking the offered paw, 'Basil Brush. Pleased to meet you.'

'Aye. I'm sure you are.' Our short conversation was interrupted when my name was called by the production assistant. It seemed I had been given preferential treatment and wouldn't have to queue like the others – much to the annoyance of Mr McPike.

Once inside, I decided to take a bit of a chance and do some new stuff at the audition. I'd put together a routine about a fictional cousin of mine:

'Cousin Dennis comes from the rich side of the family. He was born with a silver spoon in his mouth – and he hasn't stirred yet. Ha! Ha! He's a fox of rare gifts – well he's never given me one. In fact, he's so cheap he doesn't even tip his hat. He doesn't get haircuts either – every six weeks he gets his ears lowered. I have to say, he's so sneaky he wouldn't even look a potato in the eye. No one likes him. You know he actually lights up a whole room just by leaving it.' And so on . . .

Initially, the production team seemed too busy talking to one another, making notes and going out for cups of tea to pay much attention, but I did soon have them listening to me and they did all laugh when I told them about Dennis's glass eye. He used to keep it a secret until one day it came out in the conversation. Boom! Boom!

They definitely liked the Boom! Boom! business. I was also beginning to throw in the laugh that was to become one of my trademarks. I finished the act to a round of applause and left them wanting more.

Ten days, and about forty phone calls later (from me that is) Harry's producer friend got round to making contact. I'd got the job, but was going to have to share the billing with my new acquaintance, Spike McPike. The show was to be called *The Three Scampeys* and I would be given a chance to try out some of my own material.

Harry was over the moon. He came to the phone himself, telling me this was the perfect showcase for my talents. It seemed I'd finally made my breakthrough. I was in television and in the big time.

'This is your big breakthrough?' Spike smirked a few weeks later, when we were sitting chatting in the corner of a draughty rehearsal hall in Paddington, him warming himself with nips from his secret flask, me with a packet of jelly babies that I kept pressed to the radiator to catch every last morsel of heat. 'Don't hold your breath, my friend. Every time I've thought, this is the one, this'll keep me going on a roll for the rest of my career, and every one of them slipped away to nothing. Take my advice, son. Take every penny you can get out of them and buy yourself a wee pub the moment you can afford it. That'll see you through your twilight years.'

I was too excited to let Spike's world-weariness get me down. With all the confidence of youth and inexperience I went into work each day with a certainty that I was about to become a major star.

In these days of satellite, cable, video and multiple choice television, it's hard to remember that only forty years ago things were very different indeed. If you were on television you were on one of only three channels, and BBC2 was only really watched by about three people until the *Forsyte Saga* made soap operas intellectually acceptable. (I have to admit that much as I admire him as an all-round entertainer with huge talent, I wasn't sure that Bruce actually merited a mini-series.)

So now, appearing regularly on the commercial network, I was being seen by audiences of up to several million at a time! In those days, anyone who appeared on the screen soon got themselves noticed and was able to make an impact in the world of show business. From that moment on there was no doubt in my mind, it was going to be my business. The magic had entered my soul.

☆ ☆ ☆ ☆ ☆ ☆ ☆ ☆ ☆ ☆ ☆ ☆ ☆ ☆

CHAPTER FOUR
THIS HAPPY BREED

☆ ☆ ☆

'I like long walks, especially when they are taken by people who annoy me. In all the times we worked together, I never suggested even the tiniest stroll for Basil. Acting with him was simply marvellous. His wit, style and elegance left me perfectly green with envy. Always, an absolute trooper . . . apart from that terrible toffee debacle.'

Noël Coward

Life was good. I was beginning to enjoy the highlife and was having a great deal of fun sharing the Bloomsbury flat with my actor pals. I thought of it as my own Bloomsbury 'set' although I never referred to it in this way in front of my mother as she had always considered badgers rather decadent creatures with nasty habits! I was earning quite well and could afford jelly babies every night. I was even able to send money home to my parents. My television appearances on *The Three Scampeys* had been well received and the public was clamouring for more. But something even more exciting was in store: David Nixon, that marvellous magician and the Paul Daniels of his day – only without Debbie McGee – had seen my act and realized I had a lot to offer. His people contacted my people (I loved the idea of having 'people' – in reality there was only one person, my agent, Harry Burns) and asked if I would be interested in working with him. A meeting was duly arranged in Mr Burns' office with Mr Nixon and producer Johnny Downes.

Harry was, as ever, straight to the point. 'Now I'm not having Basil wearing feathers in his hair, a sequinned bodice and doing a lot of gesticulating.'

Mr Nixon dismissed the idea immediately. 'Oh no, I don't want Basil as a magician's assistant – I'd need someone with better legs. No offence, Basil.'

'None taken, Mr Nixon.' I was greatly relieved although somewhat discommoded by his remark about my legs which I had always considered rather shapely and of great support to me.

'Good,' the polished prestidigitator continued, 'I want to give you a free hand, Basil. I want you to be able to write your own stuff. I'll be your straight man and you can develop the act in any way you want. I'll give you five minutes or so in each show. It'll bring you to a whole new audience of adults, but I don't want it to be smutty or contain any innuendo.'

Harry interrupted, 'Now steady, David, Basil doesn't do that kind of material.'

I agreed. 'Harry's right. I don't know the meaning of the word "double-entendre" – either of them! Ha! Ha!'

Mr Nixon chuckled. 'That's the sort of stuff we want

but don't make it too clever – we'll be working for ITV, you know.'

Harry suggested that Mr Nixon and I went out for lunch whilst he sorted out the 'practicalities' with Mr Downes. I was more than happy with this arrangement and looked forward to spending some time with the celebrated conjuror.

That lunch was the start of a close and lasting personal and professional relationship. Mr Nixon was a Goliath. A gentle giant. He looked for all the world like the trusted family lawyer or doctor, with his sober suits and shiny bald pate, and I was able to ham up the mischievous, aristocratic side of my character. He fed me the lines and I got all the laughs.

I expect you've heard about the chap who swallowed a tin of varnish and had a lovely finish. Well, Mr Nixon always had a spectacular ending to the shows with some astounding illusion or other bringing gasps of amazement from the audience. Working with him on *The Nixon Line* was a great pleasure and he even asked me to help with a few of his illusions. He tried levitation on me but it didn't work – I just could never rise to the occasion. Boom! Boom!

David taught me a few tricks, I can tell you. Well, actually, I can't tell you or I'll have The Magic Circle after me. There is a strict code of conduct among the conjuring fraternity and no magician would ever divulge the secrets of the trade. However, I can tell you that David Nixon had so many cards up his sleeve he would send his suit to be cleaned, pressed and shuffled.

Some of the magic went out of my life when the show ended, but soon I was destined to meet another show business legend. It all began with a phone call from Harry

Burns one Friday morning just after breakfast.

'Basil? Are you busy?'

'Not especially, Harry. I was just staring at a carton of orange juice.'

'What on earth are you doing for that for?'

'It says "concentrate". Ha! Ha!'

'Yes very good but I've got no time for your little jokes and believe me, that was a very little joke. Listen to this. I've got you another job.'

Now I *was* concentrating. 'Oh yes?'

I could tell Harry was excited. 'It's a commercial.'

My heart sank. 'Harry, you know I'm not too sure about doing commercials so early in my career.'

'I know, Basil, I know.'

'The risk is that I'll compromise my comedy if I become too closely connected to a particular product. A comedian is a commentator on the frailties of mankind and needs to maintain an integrity of his own in order to point the finger of mockery at others.'

'They're going to pay you a fortune, you'll be working with Noël Coward *and* it's for toffees!'

'I'll do it.'

Harry was delighted. 'I knew you'd see sense, Basil.'

I couldn't believe my ears. 'Noël Coward is making a commercial?'

'He's starring in it.'

If Mister Noël was willing to associate his name with this venture then it was almost certainly safe for me. And what's more, toffees were second only to jelly babies in my sucking order of favourite sweets.

'They're shooting it at the Ritz tomorrow morning.'

'The Ritz Hotel? In Piccadilly?'

'Yes, they want an elegant setting that will do both you and Noël justice. Be there by seven o'clock.'

Early morning is not my best time, coming from a long line of chaps who like nothing better than to howl at the moon, but I knew it was the way these television people liked to work and this was an opportunity not to be missed.

Harry continued, 'Oh, and Basil—'

'Yes?'

'Hire a dinner jacket.'

'Of course, Harry.'

'Shine your shoes.'

'Yes, Harry.'

'Make sure you look smart.'

'All right, Harry, but please don't go on and on about what I should wear – you're going to make me clothestrophobic! Ha! Ha!'

I arrived at the Ritz in plenty of time the following morning. The front of house staff must have thought I was some sort of swell returning late from a party. They set me up with a coffee in the lobby without even asking who I was. That's the wonder of a bit of fine tailoring, people automatically assume you're a person of some importance.

None of the other artistes seemed to have arrived, although I could see the television crew assembling near the fountain in the lobby. I couldn't believe that not so long ago I'd been working in a greasy spoon to make some extra money and here I was enjoying the height of opulence in a glamorous hotel. Sort of 'out of the frying pan into the foyer'.

The hotel staff were buzzing around the extras like flies, obviously worried that they would upset the guests on their way to and from breakfast. I thought perhaps I should go over and introduce myself. I was beginning to feel a bit peckish and I suspected there was a strong possibility there might be a bacon sandwich on offer. That much I knew about film crews – they were never too far from a bacon sandwich.

As I approached them, Mister Noël himself descended the stairs and made his way towards the dining room, waving a neatly folded copy of *The Times* at the dishevelled looking man who I assumed must be the director. The man waved back, signalling that he had seen where the star was going and would therefore know where to look for him, should they need him. If they didn't yet need Noël, I decided, they didn't need me either. I gave them an identical wave, to let them know where I was going and caught up with the great man as he teetered on the threshold of the finest dining room in London, waiting for the head waiter to seat him.

'Mister Noël,' I said, stretching out a friendly paw. 'Basil. I believe we're working together today.'

'Thrilled,' he said, shaking my hand firmly. 'Would you care to join me?'

'Thrilled,' I said. I'd always believed that the sincerest form of flattery is imitation if not downright plagiarism.

'Table for two, Mr Coward?' the head waiter enquired.

'Please. But nowhere near that dreadful fountain,' Noël glanced pointedly in the direction of the extravagant water feature holding centre stage, 'I haven't brought my umbrella.'

It felt good to be at the Master's side and to be the centre of attention. Those who didn't know about the television crew lurking in the foyer obviously assumed we were travelling companions, although they might have wondered why I was in evening dress and Noël seemed to be wearing his dressing gown. I was also wondering about this but decided not to pursue the matter.

A table was finally located that Mr Noël found acceptable and soon we were tucking into a delicious breakfast. The Master dipped his spoon delicately into his lightly boiled egg and glanced at me as I wrestled with my kedgeree. 'Have you read the script, Basil?'

'Yes, I think it's rather g . . .'

'Ghastly, isn't it? "Champions Chewy Chocolate Caramels Create Constant Companionship".' His delivery was as perfect as ever. 'Alliteration is such a cheap trick, don't you think?'

'An abomination. Absolutely awful,' I replied.

Noël raised an eyebrow in a clear indication of admiration. Pleased with myself, I decided to take the plunge. 'I must say, Mister Noël, I was rather surprised that you would do a commercial for toffees.'

'I'm terribly fond of toffees. Always have been. I've got a frightfully sweet tooth. I've even written about it. Haven't you seen my revue *Cavalcade*? The original title was *Caramelcade*. Or my play, *Bitter Sweet*? What the public don't know is that it's really about chocolate. Now, Basil, it's our little secret.' The Master took his final mouthful of egg, dabbed his lips with a theatrical flourish. 'Tell me Basil, what exactly have you done?'

'You mean this morning? Well I got up at about seven, paid a quick visit, brushed my teeth—'

Mister Noël interrupted, ' I meant what work have you done?'

'Mostly television. Perhaps you've seen me?'

'Television is something you appear on, but never watch.'

'Quite, quite, I agree completely. I don't have a set myself. I prefer books, although it does get a bit boring watching a pile of novels in the corner of my living room. Ha! Ha!'

Mr Noël smiled at me knowingly and picked up an extraordinarily ornate ivory cigarette holder. I couldn't take my eyes off the astounding object which was at least three feet long.

'Ah,' I said, 'that's one way of staying away from cigarettes! Boom! Boom!'

Just then, a very well known Shakespearean actor walked past and stopped at our table. 'Basil, hello dear boy. How are you? Would love to chat, but I'm late. Breakfast meeting.' The actor winked and gestured in the direction of a glamorous blonde sitting at a table on the side of the dining room. As he made his way across to her, he shot Noël Coward a puzzled glance. 'And who's your friend?'

I was delighted to have been acknowledged so publicly, but mortified that my thespian friend had failed to recognize the Master. I decided to be upbeat. 'Dear Sir Freddie, isn't he sweet? Quite eccentric, of course, doesn't even remember who he is sometimes. Probably immersed in his present role. He's an actor. I once saw him play Hamlet.'

'And I dare say that Hamlet lost.'

'I'm really sorry, Mister Noël, that he didn't realize who you were.'

'My importance to the world is relatively small. On the other hand, my importance to myself is tremendous. It is not the eyes of others that I am wary of, but of my own. He obviously doesn't remember I had dinner with him once. A late dinner with Sir John Gielgud, Sir Ralph Richardson, Sir Laurence Olivier and Sir Donald Wolfit.'

'It must have been an all-knight restaurant. Ha! Ha!'

The master exhaled a perfect circle of smoke. 'Very droll, Basil. You're actually rather fun. But don't overdo it. Wit ought to be a um . . . er . . . oh . . . Wit ought to be . . .'

'Wit ought to be a glorious treat like caviar – never spread it about like marmalade. Boom! Boom!' I was on top form.

'That's awfully good, Basil. Would you mind terribly if I used that? Although I think it may work better for me without the "Boom! Boom!".'

'Be my guest, Mister Noël. I'd be flattered.'

'I've enjoyed this breakfast, Basil. When this dreadful business is all over, do drop in and see me at Firefly – my house in Jamaica. Now, look, there's that tiresome little man again waving at us. I think we're needed.'

The director came over whilst the camera crew messed about with lights and sound equipment. 'Mr Coward, you have just finished a splendid meal and are being served coffee. Instead of an after-dinner mint, you are given one of our toffees. At first you are somewhat dismissive but then Mr Brush leans over from the adjacent table and says, "Do try one, they're frightfully good". You decide to pop the toffee into your mouth. It is delicious and after a few seconds of glorious chewing you utter the words "Champions Chewy Chocolate Caramels Create

Constant Companionship".'

Noël stared incredulously at the director, until he flushed nervously and edged away. 'Right, right, jolly good, let's get started shall we,' he stuttered.

Between takes, after lunch, I had the opportunity for another chat with Mister Noël. 'Do you play bridge, by any chance?' he asked.

'Of course,' I replied. Well, of course this wasn't exactly true. But our family had often whiled away a wet Sunday in the den with a rumbustious game of canasta and I was sure it couldn't be so different from bridge.

'Good. Would you mind terribly making up a foursome tonight? I would have asked darling Gertie but I'm afraid she can't make it.'

'Why's that?' I asked.

'Because she's dead.' Noël took a mournful puff on his cigarette holder.

'I'd love to play,' I replied.

'Good. Shall we come to your suite?' Noël asked.

'Um . . . no . . . why don't we play in yours. It's probably easier for you.'

'Not at all. I'd quite like to see your suite.'

'It's a bit of a mess. We'd be more comfortable in your suite.'

'Oh, very well. As long as you promise me, no more suite talk.'

I laughed uproariously – not just on account of the great man's wit but also greatly relieved that I didn't have to admit to the ignominy of not actually staying in the Ritz for the duration of the shoot.

Mister Noël looked me up and down. 'I've been watching you today and I think you're wasted in this commercial. You're actually rather good. You haven't got nearly enough to do. I'm going to have a word with the director.'

'Thank you very much, Mister Noël.' I was delighted to know that my work had been appreciated by someone and by Noël Coward of all people. But then that is why we in this business, known as show, refer to him as The Master.

Mister Noël was, of course, true to his word and after lunch and some heated words with the director, I actually found myself co-starring! In an incredible act of generosity, Mister Noël even insisted that I deliver the final line of the commercial.

Unfortunately I think I over-rehearsed because by the time I was to say the immortal words, 'Champions Chewy Chocolate Caramels Create Constant Companionship' I was speechless. Not because of stage fright or temporary memory loss, it was just that, being the final take, I had tried to cram too many toffees into my mouth and at the vital moment my jaws became clamped together. Everyone was very nice and tried to prise them open but even the key grip couldn't help. I was what you might call stuck dumb.

My big chance had gone and in the end they had to make do with their original plan of Mister Noël doing the line. In fact, no one seemed too disappointed – least of all the director who was less than sympathetic about my predicament.

Once filming was all over and everyone (including me) had told Mister Noël how wonderful he was, I went upstairs to his room where he was already pouring drinks.

I'd mentioned that I had a penchant for cream soda and he had very kindly arranged a special delivery from room service with some canapés. 'It's not nearly as sparkling as you,' he said as he handed me a glass, 'but it will have to suffice.' He introduced me to a young actress who called herself Martita. I can only assume she called herself this because it was her name. She was quite stunning and I was desperate to make an impression. However, she seemed only to have eyes for Mister Noël and bombarded him with the latest gossip: 'Noël, did you hear about . . . ?' Martita mentioned the name of a very famous but equally dim actor.

'No.' Mister Noël was agog with indifference as he poured himself a glass of champagne.

'He committed suicide.'

Mister Noël looked up. 'How did he kill himself?'

'Blew his brains out.'

'He must have been a marvellous shot.'

Mister Noël then suddenly began fussing around the room plumping cushions as I chatted nonchalantly with Martita. Then, most surprisingly, a plain clothes policeman arrived and wandered around the room twitching the curtains and peering under the sofa, apparently looking for something, although he never said what. Noël seemed not to notice he was there, being obsessed with checking his hair and his tie in the mirror, both of which looked as immaculate as they had at the start of the day.

Half an hour later there was a knock at the door. Mister Noël leapt to his feet and who should enter – wait for this, dear reader – but the Queen Mother! Yes, the Queen Mother. If only my own dear old mum had been able to see this. The Q.M. made herself at home, kicked off her shoes and flopped on to the sofa, gin and tonic in hand as if she'd just got back from a hard day's labour behind a counter at Peter Jones. She was just as lovely as I'd expected: all peaches and cream wrinkles and sparkly little eyes. I think I may have looked a bit stunned for a moment or two at seeing her in full colour, so to speak, but she quickly put me at ease with that patter which all the royals do when stuck for small-talk (she would have been good in the ad, come to think of it).

I was soon to discover that it was she who was to be my bridge partner for the evening. Imagine that! If only I knew my singletons from my doubletons, my conventions from my contracts and my hearts from my elbow. Fortunately, we had burnt rubber for only a short time when, before they had time to discover I was the real dummy, the Q.M. came up with a surprising suggestion. 'Noël, this bridge lark is all very well, but I think we all know why we're here.'

The Master nodded sagely. 'I knew it would only be a matter of time.'

'Good. Let's play some real cards. Is that all right with you?' The Q.M. looked at us expectantly.

Martita nodded enthusiastically – I took her lead and for the first time that evening followed suit. 'Marvellous!'

'Marvellous!' The Q.M. set out her stall, 'Stud and draw, Texas hold 'em. No limits.'

'No limits?' I quavered. 'I'm afraid I haven't got enough cash on me for a serious . . . game,' my voice trailed off.

'Oh we never play with cash – much too vulgar.' The Q.M. emptied her handbag on to the table and several hundred chips of varying colour spilled out. 'Let's play cards.'

I noticed that Her Majesty had removed her diamond tiara and replaced it with a 'Caesar's Palace' inscribed visor. She shuffled the pack of cards with a speed and dexterity David Nixon would have envied. 'Dealer's choice. Let's start with a little seven-card stud – hi-low, a pair of tens to open, one-eyed Jacks are wild.'

We were off and I was soon in trouble. The Q.M. was an absolute demon and when she did seem to lose a hand, she always muttered something about 'household rules' and grabbed the kitty. I tried to keep up but was losing heavily.

All came to a head with the final hand of the evening. After several rounds of betting, Noël and Martita had folded and I was holding three aces – my best hand of the night. It was my only chance to recoup some of my losses. I also thought the Q.M. was bluffing because her face had reddened – a sort of 'royal flush'. I threw in my final chips.

The Q.M. threw hers dramatically in the middle and then upped the ante, 'I'll raise you Cornwall.'

I was dumbfounded. 'I'd always been led to believe that the Duchy belonged to your grandson, Prince Charles.'

'I have his marker,' the Queen Mother snapped back.

I thought this was very unfair, particularly as I had no counties at my disposal but I gave her *my* marker and insisted on 'seeing' her hand.

Her Majesty spread her cards on the table in a victorious sweep. 'Read 'em and weep. A back-door straight.'

'Ah, the face that launched a thousand chips,' a suave voice interjected.

I really didn't need Mister Noël's devastating wit at this particular time and by now I was shaking with anxiety. 'Your Majesty, I really don't quite know how I will ever pay you back.'

The Q.M. gave me a curious look. 'Don't you worry, Basil, I have your IOU. I'll call it in one day – when we're both ready.'

I had no idea what she meant but was grateful that I was not for the Tower.

Mister Noël, always the perfect host, had arranged for dinner to be served during which there was a lot of chat about the Caribbean, Noël going on about the joys of Jamaica again and the Queen Mother talking about a house Margaret had had built for herself on Mustique. They both told me I 'absolutely must' get to the Caribbean before it was completely ruined by tourists.

I absolutely agreed.

By the time we'd finished our meal, we were all congaing around the room in the greatest of style. All in all, an unforgettable evening and although it cost me a small fortune it was worth every penny.

I was to work with Noël Coward again in another commercial when we were to discover a mutual love of jelly babies. It was shot on location on Richmond Common together with about a thousand children from a well known stage school of dramatic art. Advertising executives Henry Cohen and Jack Carmen (they were so overworked at times that they didn't know whether they were Carmen or Cohen) came up with the following jingle that Mister Noël and I were supposed to sing:

There are many facets to Messrs Bassetts
Like endless hours of fun
Say yes, not maybe
To a jelly baby
And then have another one.

Although I didn't think it was bad, Mister Noël described it as drivel and flatteringly asked me to re-write the lyrics. I was delighted and came up with:

Mad dogs and Englishmen go out in the midday sun
They run the risk of rabies to find some jelly babies
The Burmese love to try them
The Chinese all stirfry them
With the greatest ease
The Singalese
Put them in a spicy stew
So if you like curry
You'd better hurry
To the nearest vindaloo.

Mister Noël was incredibly impressed and so were the agency. The commercial was a great success both artistically and financially and as an added bonus we were both given a lifetime's supply of jelly babies. It was on the shoot that the Master gave me advice that I have always tried to live by: 'Trust your instincts. If you have no instincts, trust your impulses. My dear Basil, I believe you have both in abundance.'

I was later to take up the Master's kind invitation to visit him in Jamaica – but that is another story – or at least another chapter. . .

CHAPTER FIVE
BY ROYAL COMMAND

☆ ☆ ☆

My brush goes Boom! Boom! bang-a-bang
Boom! Boom! bang-a-bang
'Cos you are here
Boom! Boom! bang-a-bang
Boom! Boom! bang-a-bang right in my ear
Thrashing away, thrashing away
Will you be true?
Boom! Boom! bang-a-bang bang I love you.

An excerpt from 'Ode to Lulu'
– Basil Brush

The year that was 1969 was extraordinarily momentous. Neil Armstrong set foot on the moon, Mr Nixon (Richard, not David) was inaugurated as President of the United States, Concorde, the supersonic airliner, made its maiden flight, John Lennon married Yoko Ono, the first episode of *Monty Python* was transmitted and the last episode of *Star Trek* was aired.

1969 was also the year I lost my heart for the first time.

I'd first met Marie McDonald McLaughlin Lawrie – or Lulu, as you and her fans all over the world know her – when I was learning to drive. I'd been for a meeting at Harry Burns' offices (a pretty significant meeting at that, and one which I will tell you about later) and had arranged for my driving instructor to pick me up from there.

I was driving along very carefully on what must have been my third or fourth lesson when I stopped at a set of traffic lights – I was always a very obedient driver. And, I have to say, confident – I managed to pass my test first time and became a rather good and responsible motorist. In fact, I was always getting compliments on my driving. I often came back to my pillarbox red Austin Healey to find a note on my windscreen that said, 'Parking Fine'.

Anyway, I digress. I was at these traffic lights and I looked over at the driver of the car next to me. A sporty little number with a wonderful chassis and a set of headlights you would die for. I'm afraid I don't remember much about the car. Anyway, this gorgeous creature looked over and I don't know what came over me but I gave her a toot on my horn and returned her look. She then tooted her horn and stared at me. I gave her 'the once over' and also another toot on my horn. She glanced at me again and pressed her horn. I winked at her and somewhat bravely gave her another toot on the horn. I can only say it was 'an eye for an eye and a toot for a toot'.

We swapped telephone numbers and before long we were seeing quite a lot of each other. I was captivated by this Scottish redhead who was quite the most vivacious vixen I'd seen in a long time. I was completely smitten. To me, she was the most beautiful thing I'd ever seen and I told her so: 'Your eyes are like blueberries, your lips are like cherries, your cheeks are like apples.' I looked at her adoringly and she replied in those dulcet Glaswegian tones, 'You make me sound more like a fruit salad than a girlfriend.'

I have to admit I wasn't terribly confident around the opposite sex in those days and often found myself a bit tongue-tied. I felt my parents were to blame; as loving as they were, they were also rather strict. I wasn't actually allowed to see a naked lightbulb until I was seventeen. Not like a cousin of mine who was very successful with the vixens and treated them all like sequels. Ha! Ha! But Miss Lulu didn't seem to mind and we were soon dancing the nights away in all of London's top night spots. For the first time in my life I was attracting some media attention and I have to admit that photographs of us together appeared in several tabloids alongside banner headlines such as, 'To Basil With Love', 'It Makes Them Want To Shout' and 'Basil's Bit of Brush.' I told her that it was a lovely feeling when I was in her arms and my heart went Boom! Boom! when she was near. She seemed to think that this was very romantic and went as far as to write it down.

Anyway, I mentioned the meeting at Harry Burns' earlier; he had moved offices to a palatial suite in Regent Street and the framed photographs on the wall now reflected his successful status. Although James Dean and Brando still remained, the snake charmers and contortionists had been replaced by well known singers and comedians. However, it was not only Mr Burns' working environment that had been transformed – so had Harry. Gone were the cricketing flannels, cravats and dyed blond hair. Now Harry possessed a colourful collection of kaftans, a myriad of bead necklaces dangled from his neck and he also sported luxuriant, jet black hair under a tie-dyed headband. It was more like visiting a guru than an agent.

Despite his ridiculous appearance, the fact that he said 'far out' a lot and made liberal use of the two-fingered peace sign, Harry had developed into a feared and respected agent with a lot of impressive clients. He seemed to be living in the lap of luxury and during our meeting was stretched out on his new crushed suede sofa.

'Bas, I've had a call from some P.A. at the Beeb. They want to see you at Television Centre. So we've set up an appointment.'

I was flattered. 'The BBC have asked to see me?'

Harry sat up, 'Well, that's not quite true. The BBC never ask for you – they send for you. And, unlike the Mafia, you cannot refuse, even if they haven't made an offer.'

'Well that sounds very exciting, I must say. Thanks Harry.'

'That's my job, man. Listen, do you want me to come with you?'

I considered it momentarily. Harry was a great negotiator, knew me well and would look after my interests but I was sometimes slightly embarrassed in his presence and I still couldn't get used to his abundant application of patchouli oil which tended to make me feel nauseous. There could be disastrous consequences – particularly in confined spaces.

'No thanks, Harry, I'd like to handle this one myself.'

'Please yourself . . .'

The meeting was on a Friday. It was pouring with rain and I took a taxi. We were caught in traffic, and as I watched the meter ticking up, I thought to myself this is money for jam. Ha! Ha!

For once, the driver wasn't the usual chirpy, wise-cracking London cabbie. He was morose and po-faced. So I decided to cheer him up. That was my first mistake. 'It's raining cats and dogs,' I said, 'and I know that because I just stepped in a poodle.' Nothing. No reaction, apart from a groan. I decided to try again. 'It may surprise you to know that I was once a taxi driver, but I had to give it up. I couldn't stand people talking behind my back. Ha! Ha!'

With one swift movement, he slammed shut the glass partition. The remainder of the journey was passed in silence, until we arrived at Television Centre, when I gave him a rather generous tip. He was obviously delighted and he finally spoke, appearing to be rather moved. 'Thanks very much, I always thought you was different from the others.'

'The others?' I queried.

'Oh yeah, I've had all you lot in the back of my cab: Lenny the Lion, Emu, Lamb Chop, but none of them was as generous as you.'

I was pleased. 'Oh well, one does what one can.'

'No straight up, mate, you've always been my favourite.'

'Well thank you very much. Here's another twenty pence. Have a cream soda on me.'

The cabbie's eyes lit up. 'Very kind. And I'll make sure

your generous act doesn't stay a secret with me. Well, I'd best be off. Work to be done. Cheers Sooty!'

Before I could say a word, he had driven off, smiling happily. Oh well, I thought to myself, at least Sooty's reputation would be enhanced and, like Harry Corbett, I could say I had a hand in it.

I approached the barrier with some confidence – let's face it, it was the only way to deal with those commissionaires on the gate (I'm sure I recognized one of them from Frinton) – and before long I was actually in Television Centre. The atmosphere was quite congenial, and I realized how much they look after themselves at the BBC. Plush wall-to-wall carpeting, subtle pink lights and soft background music, the odd potted plant. And that was only the lift.

On the top floor I walked down the corridors of power, although I must say there was an underlying sense of fear and insecurity. This was confirmed when I arrived at the senior executive's door. His name was written in chalk, and there was a damp rag hanging beside it. I knocked at the door and it was opened by a craggy-faced, bearded figure who peered at me suspiciously. Reassured by my best smile, he ushered me into a sumptuous room and offered me a limp hand to shake, reminding me I must replenish my stock of jelly babies. Then he sat behind a giant desk and peered over the top of his spectacles.

'Glad you could make it, Mr Brush. Underground crowded, was it?'

'No, you see I came . . .' I swallowed my words. If it pleased him to feel superior, then I'd go along with it. And, in fact, turn it to my advantage. 'Yes, we were jam-packed together – I've never had so much fun without laughing.'

He didn't. He just looked smug and gave me a sardonic smile which I assumed was caused by eating too many sardines. 'As you probably know, I'm with the Department of Light Entertainment.' His manner was anything but 'light'. He was pompous, overbearing and undoubtedly wanted me to feel I was in the presence of a corporation big-wig. Personally, I wouldn't have guessed he was a big-wig, except that, occasionally, it would slip down over his eyes.

'Now, I understand that you have some television experience?'

'Yes, it was on the other channel.'

'What other channel?' He laughed uproariously at his own joke, rocked back in his chair and fell into the drinks cabinet where, I have to say, he looked quite at home. A few bottles had fallen into his lap and I couldn't resist saying, 'That's probably the first time the drinks have been on you.' He managed a weak smile as he extricated himself. Then he put a bottle of champagne in the ice bucket and said, 'That should be chilled nicely by the time you've gone. I've been hearing all about you from some of my colleagues – but in spite of that we'd like to offer you your own show.'

Well, I hadn't been in the business that long but I knew enough not to wear my heart on my sleeve. Especially when playing poker. Never show your hand. Don't be over enthusiastic. Show a lack of interest. Be laid back. Play it cool. I jumped off my chair. 'When do we start?' Second mistake today.

He sniggered scornfully, 'That's just wiped a few grand off your fee.'

'I don't think so,' I snapped, recovering, 'I'll get my

agent up here to see you. It's Harry Burns.'

The walls of his office were white and, suddenly, his face disappeared as they sort of merged. 'Oh . . . Harry Burns . . .' was all he could manage.

After rather a long pause, I said briskly, 'Well, I'd better be going. It's rush hour, and you know how crowded the tube gets.'

He picked up the phone. 'I'd better get you a car. Hello, I want a V.I.P. car immediately. Yes, for a Mister Basil Brush. Sorry, make that for *the* Mister Basil Brush.' He smiled. 'Five minutes – in front of the building.'

He hurriedly showed me to the door and retreated, as quickly, back into his office (and probably his drinks cabinet), closing the door behind him. As I left, in a parting gesture, I wiped his name off the door with the damp rag.

The following day, Harry invited me over for dinner at his house to discuss the BBC offer. This was the Cheyne Walk mansion that he'd recently bought and had just finished doing up, or, at least, his decorators had. It was very striking, pretty startling actually, all purples and reds, acres of crushed velvet, dim lighting, bowls of feather plumes and joss sticks at every turn. A bit like I imagine a harem might have been in ancient Istanbul. Through the high windows I could see the lights of the passing boats twinkling on the Thames. Here I was, sitting at the very epicentre of Chelsea, the most happening place in the world at that moment in time.

Harry was going out with a model called Twinky, an extraordinary looking woman, six feet tall and rather statuesque. She moved around the almost empty house in a cloud of sweet smelling smoke, wearing a full-length piece of see-through chiffon. Harry had obviously hoped she'd cook dinner for us, but in the end he had to order it in from one of the fashionable trattorias in the King's Road. It was quite apparent that Twinky was not someone to completely trust with a pan of boiling water.

'I've been on to the BBC already. The deal's in the bag, man. They're giving you pretty much carte blanche as to the format,' Harry was saying, although it was quite hard to hear above the thump of Pink Floyd which was emitting from Twinky's record player – the only thing she seemed to have got round to unpacking.

'I'll need a straight man,' I said. 'Someone to take over from David Nixon.'

'Anyone in mind?' Harry asked as Twinky put her arms around me and coaxed me out into the middle of the polished parquet floor to dance with her. I looked at Mr Burns slightly nervously but he nodded that it was okay.

'I've had quite a few ideas,' I shouted back, as she weaved around me, waving her arms like some Indian goddess, causing waterfalls of chiffon to rain down on my head. 'It has to be someone with impeccable comic timing – a straight actor who can do comedy.'

'I agree.' Harry had lit a home-rolled cigarette the size of a small trumpet which was sending showers of sparks over his crushed blackberry velvet bell-bottoms. 'What about Richard Briers? He's up and coming.'

'Possibly. I was wondering Rodney Bewes. He seems like a nice chap, someone I could work with.'

'Let's find his agent.'

So, as Pink Floyd became Hendrix, and Twinky continued to slide me around the parquet and the black waters of the Thames flowed silently by outside, Harry started making phone calls. By three o'clock that morning he had got someone out of bed who was able to promise – rather grumpily – that they could put him in contact with Rodney Bewes the following day.

Rodney and I hit it off straight away and filming the show hardly seemed like work at all. We'd have two or three special guests each week, people I actually wanted to meet, but I would write scripts for them, using them as foils for jokes, much as Morecambe and Wise did to great acclaim.

After the guest appearances on each show I would sit with Rodney Bewes and he would read me a story, much as my dad had done when I was a cub. I would write the stories and they would be about some character or other who was also called Basil. I couldn't help interrupting with jokes and funny asides and eventually Rodney would be unable to stand it any more and would hold my snout shut in order to silence me and finish the story.

Thankfully the public loved the show and one moment I was a minority cult figure – a sort of Lenny Bruce meets Lenny the Lion – the next moment I was a bit of a celebrity. My poster nestled on the walls of young girls' bedrooms, somewhere between Che Guevara and Jimi Hendrix. Having always been a great Hank Marvin fan myself, I found some of Jimi's guitar melodies a little hard to hum, but he always had the most exquisite good manners, enormous charisma and usually had the arm of a gorgeous 'dolly bird' as we used to describe crumpet in those days (rather disrespectfully I always thought).

In fact it was me who inspired Hendrix to write 'Foxy

Lady'. I was sitting with Miss Lulu at some club, when Hendrix passed by and I commented, rather more loudly than I had intended, on his lovely companion.

'What did you say?' he asked, narrowing his eyes through the clouds of smoke that always seemed to be leaking from his nostrils.

'I said your girlfriend was a foxy lady,' I repeated a little nervously, hoping that I hadn't given the wild man of pop cause for offence.

A slow smile spread across his face, allowing more wreaths of smoke to drift towards the ceiling and he let out a gentle chuckle, slapping his thigh in pleasure. A few weeks later I heard my words coming out of the radio in another classic Hendrix lyric.

In fact, Lulu introduced me to lots of pop stars: the Rolling Stones, the Beatles, the Pretty Things and Herman's Hermits. She also decided to mould my fashion sense, introducing me to a young tailor called Tommy Nutter who re-modelled my wardrobe. His carpentry never was much good, but he certainly knew how to design 'fab gear'. (Of course, I always insisted on keeping the same clothes for the act.)This was a time of revolution in men's clothes; Mick Jagger wore a dress at his concert in Hyde Park and Tony Snowdon was constantly being turned away by the doormen at the Ritz for wearing a polo neck instead of a tie. We were smashing down all the barriers, throwing over the barricades of prejudice, breaking all the rules. We just didn't care.

Then, just as it seemed as if my life couldn't get any better, it almost fell apart completely. Miss Lulu and I were enjoying a romantic candelit dinner at Le Caprice before going on to see Danny La Rue's club (it was a good job I spoke fluent French in those days) when the Scottish songstress, her eyes welling up with tears, grasped both my paws in an affectionate clinch. 'Basil, I've got something to tell you.'

'Go ahead, my dear.'

'You know I care for you a great deal, Basil, but lately I've hardly seen you. You seem distant, and, well, I thought you'd gone off me.'

'Of course I haven't. I've just been so busy with everything going on.'

'Basil, listen. I've always been honest with you. I'll get straight to the point. I've met someone else. We're in love and we're going to be married.'

'Who is it?' I gasped.

'It doesn't matter.'

'Well, it does to me – and probably to him. Please tell me, Miss Lulu.'

'It's Maurice Gibb – he's one of the Bee Gees.'

I was shocked and yet it was all so obvious now. Miss Lulu had been singing 'Shout' in an usually high-pitched voice recently. I suppose I'd only got myself to blame – with all the writing and performing of the show I'd been less than attentive. I have to admit that I had been neglecting her during these heady days.

Miss Lulu kissed me gently on the snout. 'I'm so sorry Basil. The last thing I wanted to do was hurt you.'

I was devastated. I just couldn't look Miss Lulu in the face and my eyes drifted over her shoulder and into the misty distance. I didn't know what to say or what to do. Then I focussed on a table in the corner, behind Miss Lulu, where a solitary figure sat nibbling some cheesecake. A beautiful figure. The beautiful, solitary figure of none other than Miss Sandie Shaw. An *outright* Eurovision Song Contest Winner.

Miss Lulu was becoming upset – surprisingly so as she was the one dumping me. 'I can't bear this, Basil. Please say something. Anything.'

'That's okay, Miss Lulu, these things happen.' I smiled reassuringly at the dear girl, before my eyes drifted back to the natural loveliness of Miss Shaw. In something of a trance I stood up from the table. 'Goodbye, Lulu. It was wonderful while it lasted.'

Miss Lulu was amazed. 'Is that it? Is that all you have to say?'

'Well, perhaps if you wouldn't mind picking up the bill, in the circumstances, I'd be very grateful.'

I walked casually towards Miss Shaw, resisting the temptation to throw myself at her bare feet, and sitting down elegantly opposite her said, 'H-e-l-l-o, my name's Basil. Could I be your next puppet on a string?'

To theatre people, especially in the world of variety, the Palladium is something special. You walk on to its stage, and there is a certain magic. You sense it, you feel it. It helps to give you the old razzle-dazzle. That's why the greatest performers in the world love 'playing the Palladium'. And when I was there myself, I met most of them. I won't list them because it would sound like name dropping – and if there's one thing I hate, it's name dropping. I was only saying that to Prince Charles the other evening.

The theatre's variety shows and, indeed, the televised Sunday night shows gave an opportunity to so many of those brilliant speciality acts. Acrobats, jugglers, magicians, comedy dancers, knife-throwing acts and so forth. I haven't mentioned fire-eaters because, well, you need a flare for that sort of thing. Ha! Ha! Alas, all these acts seem to have vanished since there are no longer the venues for them to perform. There was one speciality act who invited me to join them in a little experiment. The 'hit man' was going to shoot a cigarette out of my mouth – blindfolded. 'Sorry, I'd love to be in the act, but I can't help you,' I said craftily, 'I don't smoke.'

Then, of course, the Palladium became home to the Royal Variety Show, the annual glittering event in which I had the privilege to appear on more than one occasion. Behind the scenes there was always a buzz of excitement, and a great camaraderie among the artistes. In spite of certain personal rivalries, an air of bonhomie was prominent. Much joking and laughter helped first night nerves. Of course, it was like a first night. It was also like the last night. I once opened my act by saying, 'After all these years in the business, I end up doing a one-night stand. Ha! Ha!'

The show was always held on a Monday and admitted only the high priced ticket holders, resplendent in evening attire, bedecked with diamond-studded tiaras, rings, bracelets, earrings and necklaces. And that was only the men! One of the comperes, singer and comedian Norman Vaughan, observed, 'No need to worry about burglars tonight, you've got it all with you.' Personally, I'd never seen so much dazzling headwear, and decided that there must be a tiara-boom today! Tiara Boom! Boom! today perhaps!

Now when you've done a good show, you go to the

dressing room and relax. On a Royal Variety show, it's different. The Queen and royal party always come backstage and the acts all line up to be presented.

I remember waiting backstage to meet the Queen for the very first time. It was a star studded line-up and I couldn't help thinking that if Harry Burns had been present he would have been totting up the combined value of all those in the show, working out the percentage of commission were he to handle them all. And I'm quite sure his eyes would have lit up and said, 'tilt'. Ha! Ha!

As the big moment approached we were all fidgeting. The ladies adjusted their hair, clothes and make-up. The men looked surreptitiously downwards. What's the protocol? We had been briefed. Don't speak unless you're spoken to. Suddenly, the chit chat ceased. They were coming. Out of the corner of my eye I could see the great impresario Bernard Delfont moving down the line. Well I wasn't going to bow to him. Grovel definitely. Ha! Ha! Then there was a great hush. The Queen got nearer.

Next to me stood the fabulous Dickie Henderson, who I so greatly admired. Out of the corner of his mouth, he said to me, 'Basil, don't forget – kneel, and you might get a knighthood. Put your head down and you might get executed.' I managed one 'Ha—'.

The Royal party were very close. I could hear Her Majesty's comments, 'Enjoyed your performance', 'Splendid show', 'You were frightfully good.' Then she arrived in front of me. I was amazed when she leaned forward, clasped my hand and whispered in my ear, 'Mother hasn't forgotten you still owe her. You will be hearing from her shortly . . .'

I smiled weakly and muttered, 'Of course, Ma'am, I

look forward to it.' But the Queen had moved on and I'd forgotten to emulate the great Tommy Cooper. Do you remember the time at one of these bashes when he asked Her Majesty whether she liked football? 'No,' replied the Queen. 'Good,' was Tommy Cooper's response. 'Could I please have your Cup Final tickets then?'

Luckily there'd been a bit of a lull in the proceedings while I'd been thinking back on this. Where was Prince Philip? Oh, there, way down the line, still talking to the dancing girls. I thought, yes, of course, he's a naval man, he'll be happier with a hand on the Tiller. Boom! Boom!

I continued to ponder about what Her Majesty had said about the Queen Mother. What could she have possibly have meant about 'being in touch'? Despite recent success, I couldn't possibly begin to repay the amount of money that I owed her. I supposed I would just have to wait for the next Royal Command.

CHAPTER SIX

THE NAME'S BRUSH, BASIL BRUSH

'Until recently, I had considered Sean Connery and Pierce Brosnan the most delectable things on two legs. Now that I've met Basil, he is by far the most gorgeous thing on four legs. With his urbane charm, panache and ability never to be shaken nor stirred, Basil would have made the perfect Bond.'
Plenty Galore, Bond Girl

Once we'd finished filming the first series of my show, whilst I had a break in my schedules – more telly work was on its way – I decided to take up Mister Noël's kind invitation to visit him in Jamaica.

Yes, I certainly was going up in the world – about

thirty-five thousand feet to be exact – and here I was on
board a jumbo jet bound for the exotic Caribbean. I'd
never flown before and I could hardly contain my excitement as I turned to the lady in the seat next to me. 'Look
at those people down there – they look like ants!'

'They *are* ants, we haven't taken off yet,' she barked as
she fastened her seatbelt with aplomb. Why she didn't use
her hands, I don't know. Ha! Ha! Anyway, with that little
faux-paw behind me, I settled down to enjoy the flight and
the thought that, on landing, Mister Noël would be there
to welcome me to the island that he – and everyone else
come to that – calls Jamaica.

If we ever got there! After three hours, our most
charming air hostess, Nikki from Croydon, told me that
we were still only half way across the pond (how long is it
going to take to fly over the Atlantic, then, I wondered?) so
I decided to lead the passengers in a spot of much-needed
community singing. No sooner had the opening strains of
'A Wandering Minstrel I' left my lips when I heard a
man's voice behind me. 'Pssst!'

What a nerve! Nothing but complimentary cream
soda had passed my lips since Heathrow! I ignored the
individual and continued but the voice persisted in pssst-
ing me. It was like trying to sing with someone blowing
up a bicycle tyre in your lughole. It's just not done to
interrupt a chap when he's in mid song so I was left with
no alternative: I decided to give him a severe dose of
the old 'Eye Of The Fox' treatment. I had learned this
brutal technique – a disdainfully raised eyebrow accompanied by a hard stare – from my Aunt Hermione who
had used it with great success for years. 'The Eye'
enabled her to jump queues, stop traffic and, on one

occasion, foil a bank robbery in the mean streets of Chipping Norton.

I turned round to let the unsuspecting wretch have it. Be afraid stranger, be very afraid!

'Would you like a hankie?' he said. 'It looks as if you're going to sneeze.'

'I'm giving you the dreaded "Eye Of The Fox" treatment.'

'Oh. Sorry.'

If I say so myself, I can hold a tune. I can hold a candle and I can hold forth. But one thing I cannot hold is a grudge. He had apologized nicely so I let the matter rest. But he wasn't finished with me. He leaned forward and whispered, 'I need to speak with you urgently on a matter of the utmost global importance.'

'The New Seekers aren't reforming, are they?' I whispered back excitedly.

'No . . .'

'The world isn't ready for them again. In fact the world wasn't ready for them the first time. Boom! Boom!'

'Boom boom is what will happen to the world if you don't agree to help us, Basil.'

'Basil!' I tell you, I get recognized everywhere these days. I must buy a pair of dark glasses!

The mysterious stranger continued, 'You see we know all about you. The woman we can only refer to as Queen Elizabeth The Queen Mother has told us all about you. That's why we are confident you will help us. After we have landed at Kingston, you will proceed to the newspaper stand by the taxi rank. Once there, you will idly peruse a copy of the *Jamaican Weekly Gleaner* until you are approached by a man wearing a straw hat named Sidney.'

'Funny name for a straw hat!' I was working well despite the mounting intrigue.

'He is one of our most trusted operatives. Whilst you're waiting for him, it is most important that you look as if you know nothing.'

That should be easy. I didn't. 'I'm sure old Sid is a smashing chap but actually, someone else is meeting me at the airport – none other than Mister Noël Coward.'

'*Was* going to meet you.' He handed me a note, indicating that I should read it in the privacy of the toilet. Life takes some funny turns, doesn't it? If you had said to me a few years ago that one day there I would be, reading a handwritten note from Noël Coward in a toilet thirty-five thousand feet up in the air, I would have been disinclined to believe you. The note made interesting if baffling reading:

My Dear Basil,

By now you will know that vital matters have conspired against our meeting as planned. What awaits will test your every nerve and sinew. It will be beastly, ghastly and terribly frightful. But where could the security of the entire world be better placed than on those small but plucky shoulders of yours? I know you will tackle your mission according to the finest traditions of The Service even if it requires the ultimate sacrifice of laying down your life for the cause. ['Laying down my life'? I should cocoa!] But who can predict which way the fickle finger of fate will point? Should you, by some chance, live to tell the tale, feel free to drop in for a quick sherbet on your way home.

Yours ever, Noël.

P.S. The Queen Mum sends her regards and says that should you pull it off, she'll tear up that IOU. And there may well be a gong in it for you.

A gong? What good was *that* going to do me? Still, I had to admit that losing my gambling debts was a tempting proposition. But what was 'the mission' Mister Noël had referred to? I returned to my seat and another round of whispering. 'What is all this about?'

'Let us just say that you will be working on something very close to your heart. We have not had this conversation.'

What had we been doing for the last five minutes, then? I reflected that if *he* was anything to go by, the people I was going to be working with were not exactly tops in the old brains department. Before sitting back in his seat and burying himself in a copy of *What Spy Camera?* magazine, he grabbed Mister Noël's note and ate it. I know the airline food was bad but that was ridiculous!

'Operative' Sidney turned out to be a chap of few words. I was just reading a small ad in the *Gleaner* for 'Miss Jenny's Hawaiian Lua Lua Club – Grass Skirts Re-Seeded While-U-Wait', when I felt a tug on my sleeve. Seconds later I was holding on for dear life as we belted at break neck speed through the back streets of Kingston in his souped-up bubble car.

I was feeling like soup myself – chicken, to be exact. 'Do you have to drive this fast?'

'Uh huh!'

Those comforting words were the last I got out of Mister Sid until we pulled up at his place on the other side of the bay, a charming beachside shed nestling in the lee of a small island occupied by a nuclear power station. Waiting for us there was a strange elderly cove named 'Q' whom I took at first to be a rather unusual travelling salesman.

'Now this little gadget looks like a conventional comb,' he said proudly.

'Never use a comb, sorry.'

'This one you *will* use.'

'I don't think so. I'd rather have a gong, if anything.'

'The whole point of my inventions is that they look like the sort of thing you would normally have on you. Why would you be carrying a gong around?'

'I don't know – but the Queen Mother wants to give me one.'

'Forget about the gong and concentrate on the comb.'

I muttered something I had once heard Mister David say when he was waiting to go on at the Television Theatre and got his magic wand caught on one of his coloured handkerchiefs. It did no good.

'Look – each one of these teeth has a range of a hundred feet. Just point the comb, squeeze and . . .'

There was a bang as one of the teeth ignited, shot out of the comb . . . and hit Mister 'Q' slap in the middle of his big toe. He let out a yelp and muttered something he had just heard *me* say. Then out of a clear blue sky fluttered . . . a parachutist. It was the mysterious stranger from the plane. He must have been flying 'economy'! Boom! Boom!

I soon realized that he was in charge of this whole daft business – whatever it was – when he came over and said,

'My name is "M" and I am in charge of this whole daft business.'

'Why didn't you say that in our previous conversation?'

'We have had no previous conversation.'

'If you say so.' There was obviously no improvement in the chap's brain power.

'Who do you all work for?' I asked, wondering who on earth would employ an operative whose contribution to the art of conversation was an occasional grunt; a boffin who shoots himself in the foot with a comb; and a boss who doesn't know what he's talking about from one moment to the next.

'British Intelligence,' said Mister 'M'. That explains a lot, doesn't it! He continued: 'I am conferring upon you double 0 status.'

'Good, I like playing with trains.'

'Which means, 008, that you are licensed to kill.'

'Kill?' I swallowed hard. 'Whom?' In spite of everything, I maintained my grammar.

'If necessary . . . one Doctor Dough.'

'Doctor Dough? Who's he?'

'He is the evil genius behind a scheme to bring the entire world to its knees. Do you see that collection of buildings on the island over there? What does it look like to you?'

'A nuclear power station.'

'It may look like a simple nuclear power station but we believe that behind that innocent façade is a top secret laboratory for producing confectionary on an undreamed of scale.'

'Confectionary?' My ears began to prick up – and then pick up *The Archers* on Radio Four, but that's another story.

At last, I was interested in what Mister 'M' was saying. 'C'mon, c'mon!'

'Your predecessor, 007, believed that Doctor Dough intends to flood world markets with cheap fairy cakes, midget gems, iced buns and the like, thereby destabilizing the global economy and rendering the entire world vulnerable to any demands he may care to make.'

'The swine!' (With all due apologies to my many pig friends.)

'Indeed. We want you, as England's foremost expert on cakes, bikkies – in fact scoffie of all kinds – to carry on where 007 left off.'

'What happened to him?'

'He fell into a vat of bun mix.'

'And?'

'He was iced. Boom! Boom!'

'I do the jokes – and that's *my* catchphrase, if you don't mind!' But I was whistling in the dark. Mister 'M''s words had struck horror into my soul, terror into my heart and fear into my mind. Being 008 was going to be almost as bad as going on first house at Frinton!

'What do you want me to do?' I asked.

'Doctor Dough has a weakness for opera. Do you, by any chance?'

'Funny you should mention that, I was talking about it with my agent not long ago and what I said . . .'

'Oh, never mind. Tonight, Doctor Dough is attending a gala performance of *Rigoletto* at the Opera House. So will you. He will be sitting in a box overlooking the stage and he will be accompanied by his lady friend, a beauty by the name of Honey Bun. She is another of his weaknesses – his Achilles' heel so to speak. You will contrive to meet her at the interval and impress her with your suave, sophisticated persona and good looks.'

I was beginning to warm to Mister 'M'. He had more brains than I first thought. He went on: 'If you impress her sufficiently, she will almost certainly invite you back to her suite at the Power Station for a quick cream soda. Once there, you will drug her with a Belgian chocolate prepared by 'Q' and then seek out Dough's inner sanctum. Your mission is to completely destroy his cake, bun and bikkie-making capability.'

'Crumbs!'

Mister 'M' was not amused. 'And, if necessary, Doctor Dough himself. Hopefully for you and the world, the story will have a better outcome than that experienced by 007.'

Doesn't he go on? Still, I liked the sound of this Miss Honey. He had one last point to make: 'And, 008, once you arrive at the opera, you will be quite on your own. We have not had this conversation.'

He was at it again, the poor chap. After a quick handshake, he and Mister 'Q' were gone. So I knew what my mission was. The future of buns – and the world – was in my paws.

That evening, Mister Sid was my dresser for what would have to be the performance of my life. He was quite chatty as he handed me the various items of clothing in which I would strut my stuff at the opera.

'White tuxedo.'

'That's awfully nice.' I put it on.

'Black tie.'

'Very tasteful.' Many years of practice had perfected my tie-tying technique. After only half an hour or so, I had it arranged perfectly.

'Cuban-heeled boots.'

'Super.' I was beginning to look cool, if I say so myself.

'Cummerbund.'

'Not before dinner!' Ah, that was a good one. Laugh? I thought Mister 'S' would never start.

'Shades.'

'Excellent.'

'Comb and chocolate.'

Oh well, I supposed I'd better show willing. I put Mister 'Q''s items in my pocket and examined myself in the mirror. I'd never looked so washed and brushed up. Brushed up! Get it?

Well, I must say, I turned quite a few heads as Mister Sid dropped me off at the theatre. It's not everyone who arrives at the opera in a chauffeur-driven bubble car. I timed my arrival – just before the overture so everyone would catch my entrance – to perfection. Mister Noël, the Master himself, would have been proud of me as, resplendent in white tux, cummerbund and shades, I strolled nonchalantly toward my seat. Perhaps the effect of debonair sophistication was slightly spoiled by my falling head first into the orchestra pit en route (those wretched sunglasses!) but I contented myself with the thought that Miss Honey may have been powdering her nose at the time and missed the incident.

Whilst they repaired the kettledrums and cymbals, I took the opportunity to scan the boxes for my quarry. Talk about poacher turned gamekeeper! I saw Doctor Dough first. What an ugly brute! Wild staring eyes, slobbering mouth, pointy twisted horns. I was just reflecting that you hardly ever see a chap with horns nowadays when I realized that I was looking at one of the plaster gargoyles that decorate the theatre. That's it – the shades are coming off! I'll just have to fascinate Miss Honey with the old baby browns when the time comes.

Doctor Dough himself proved to be an improvement on the gargoyle – but only just. By way of description, let's just say that at first I thought he was wearing a stocking over his enormous bald head. Pity the Persian cat that was sitting on his knee. And pity Miss Honey who at that moment leaned forward to give said exotic moggy a stroke.

I shall not detain you with a description of Miss Honey at this stage except to say that she was an absolute belting corker in all respects. So much so, in fact, that I let out an involuntary howl at the sight of her. Bit of 'a howler', you could say.

Although this latest gaffe was probably not in keeping with my new image, it had the excellent effect of drawing Miss Honey's peepers in my direction. I smiled as urbanely as possible under the circumstances and this seemed to do the trick. As the lights dimmed a few moments later and the overture finally got under way, a note in the form of a paper aeroplane came floating down from Doctor Dough's box. It read:

Meet me behind the rubber plant in the foyer at
the interval.
Honey

Bingo! I could hardly wait. But wait I had to – for what seemed an age. I know now why they called the show *Rigoletto*. You spend all your time wriggling in your seat waiting for the thing to stop! Apart from that, I had no idea what was going on. The action began with a party in a palace where the guests, including a hunchback 'dwarf' (who stood at least six foot three), seemed to do nothing but hurtle around the stage mocking each other. Yes, it was the Mock Hurtle Song! Then the chap in charge seemed to go round banishing people or something and then the whole thing got even more confusing. There wasn't a tune anything like as good as 'A Wandering Minstrel I' which I kindly sang to those around me during the less hectic passages.

Finally the moment I'd been waiting for arrived. The singers stopped yowling their heads off and I sidled out to the foyer to meet Miss Honey. I took up my position behind the rubber plant and waited. After just a few moments, I felt a touch on my shoulder. I turned. It was Miss Honey. In a trice, her peaches and cream complexion had turned my legs to jelly and custard. Yes, I was a trifle weak at the knees!

It was a wonderful dress that she was almost wearing. It would be lovelier still when it was finished.

'You interest me, Mister . . . ?'

'Brush. Basil Brush.'

'And what do you do?'

'About ninety in my Austin Healey. The rest is up to you.' I could see my suave spy-type banter was doing its stuff. Miss Honey felt the lapel of my tuxedo – a little too forward if you ask me – and said, 'You're sharp, like the cut of this jacket. Milan?'

'Bloomsbury.'

'It sounds . . . exotic.'

Hmm. Miss Honey may have been stunning in the looks department but she wasn't exactly The Brain Of

Kingston. She leaned forward – she always seemed to be leaning forward for some reason – and whispered in my shell-like, 'We shall go back to my penthouse suite at the power station without delay.' Sounds like she was getting ideas above her station! Ha! Ha!

'But what about your chum – old Dough Features?' As soon as I said it, I worried that my mask may have slipped but Miss Honey didn't seem to notice.

'He will stay to the end of the opera. And when he returns to the station, he has top secret production work to undertake.'

'Production of nuclear power?'

'Fondant Fancies —' my brilliant cross-examination had wormed it out of her! '—which is his pet name for strontium 90.'

That feeble attempt at covering her tracks hadn't fooled me. Doctor Dough would be working in his lair tonight. And it was there that his Fancy plans – Fondant or otherwise – were going to come to a sticky end!

After an invigorating speedboat ride round to the power station's private dock, I soon found myself in Miss Honey's suite which was all soft lights, mood music, and leopardskin upholstery. With what could only be described as abandon, she threw off her wellies and sou' wester – it had been a rough crossing – and sashayed over to the cocktail cabinet. 'Drink?'

I was feeling reckless. 'Dandelion and burdock. Shaken not stirred.'

I scanned the room purposefully. On the way up to her suite, I had kept my eyes peeled for a likely route to the sinister Doctor's inner sanctum as I hadn't the faintest idea where it was – no luck. I wondered if I could trick Miss

Honey into spilling the beans as I took my D and B. 'I don't wish to be rude, Miss Honey, but I aren't half peckish. Point me in the right direction and I'll fetch myself a few fairy cakes, ginger nuts or something.' Cunning as a fox I am sometimes!

'This is no time for ginger nuts,' she cried passionately. Dash!

She came closer. 'You fascinate me, Basil.'

Frankly, I was getting a bit fed up of Miss Honey. Up close, she was nowhere near as alluring as Miss Lulu. But it *was* thanks to her that I was on the island and for that I decided she deserved a little present. 'Fancy a chocolate?' Clever boy, Basil! I rummaged in my pocket.

'Not now.' She came even closer. 'I never could resist a man with a hairy chest . . . legs . . . and paws.'

'Do have a choc,' I said, proffering the foil-wrapped goodie. She batted it away. Dash again! If it hadn't been wrapped, I could have just stuck it in her mouth and scarpered. Yes, it was definitely a case of foiled again. Boom! Boom!

Then a funny look came into her eyes. 'Kiss me, you handsome dog.'

'Dog?!' That did it! What a cheek! Knock out drops may have their place but sometimes a short sharp rabbit punch is the only answer. Of course, I am far too much of a gentleman to do such a thing to a lady – so I decked her with a swift right Milky Way instead.

Five minutes later, after following corridor after corridor, staircase after staircase, I finally found my way . . . back to the dock. Just when I was thinking I would never find my objective, let alone destroy it, I had a whopping great stroke of luck. A freighter drew into the dock and moored up. An army of workers appeared from nowhere and started taking off its cargo: crates labelled 'Spent Fuel Rods – Danger'. If they were fuel rods, I'd eat my or anybody else's hat. I prised off one of the crate lids. Eureka! Inside was a huge stack of bun cases. I climbed inside and replaced the lid as best I could. Five minutes later, I was enjoying an (albeit cramped) sedan chair ride right into the heart of Doctor Dough's nerve centre!

Once the crate had been plonked down, I waited until all was quiet. Then I lifted the lid a crack. I could hardly believe my eyes. Although only a few lights had been left on, I could make out that I was in a vast underground cavern full of enormous vats, mixers and storage bins that must have contained thousands of tons of cake, bikkie and bun mix. A network of chutes and conveyor belts linked the whole thing to railway tracks that disappeared into a tunnel that seemed miles away in the distance. 'I wonder if you have to change to get to Oxford Circus?' I quipped. I was so nervous, I was talking to myself now!

But I was on a mission. And I could see my objective. A spiral staircase led to a gantry high above the floor. On it, a bank of computers and other control equipment hummed menacingly. That was where I should be able to wreak some havoc!

In seconds I was out of the crate, up the stairs and furiously scanning the rows of screens, dials, levers and flashing lights – one of which might help me in my task. I suppose it was too much to hope for to find a button labelled: 'Press This To Destroy The Evil Genius' Diabolical Bun Factory' – but you get the picture.

Suddenly, I heard a loud metallic thunk and the whole area was bathed in light. I spun round. There at the far

'W-e-l-l, h-e-l-l-o . . .'

Mater

Pater

Later. Ha! Ha! This is me
at Reynard High.

'Misters . . . Misters . . .
There never were
such devoted Misters.'
Recognize them?
Well, there's Mister
Rodney, Mister
Derek, Mister Roy,
Mister Billy and
Mister Howard.

The First Noel. Here, the Master is transfixed whilst yours truly (sadly out of shot) dazzles him with yet another sparkling anecdote.

And this is – no, not me but Fred. Uncanny, isn't it?

Her Majesty the Queen Mother raises her goblet of cream soda at one of our televised charity poker games. She once raised me the Duchy of Cornwall in another game that got a bit out of hand.

A Brush with romance. Ha! Ha!

The beautiful Goldie Hawn.

The lovely Lulu.

My little Maylene.

Above: I'm ready for my close up. Here's me at the Oscars. **Left:** At first I dressed rather too formally for surfing. **Below:** Pumping iron, I soon developed muscles in places I didn't know I had muscles.

Above: Do I like Las Vegas? You bet!
Right: 'Hello, Mr Chips' Ha! Ha!
Below: I still say the dancers were too tall!
This is the finale of my Las Vegas show.

Left holding the
babies! Ha! Ha!

end of the gantry stood the evil Doctor Dough, stroking his cat. He looked calm but vicious – the Doctor I mean, not the cat, although I must say I wasn't exactly struck on the pampered feline either.

'We meet at last, Mister Brush.'

'At last'? I'd never even heard of Doctor Dough until today but this seems to be how evil geniuses and secret agents prattle on so I came back with: 'We do indeed, Doctor. Quite a little bakery you have here.'

'When full production begins next week, my buns will cover the world!'

'You shouldn't have eaten so many lardy cakes!'

'You disappoint me Mister Brush. Or should I say 008. Your predecessor, 007, was much wittier.'

Cheek! But I'd get a rise out of Dough yet. Ha! Ha! You've got to hand it to me – face to face with an evil monster and still working well!

I countered: 'I disappoint nobody except my accountant and one or two aunts on my mother's side.' That showed him!

He looked puzzled and changed tack. 'I expect you're wondering how one man could have built this mighty empire.'

'Well, now that you mention it.' All the time I was verbally fencing with Dough, I was jetting sideways glances at the various control panels hoping to find *the* button.

'The answer is that I didn't achieve it alone. I work for an organization called Total World Eminence through Revolting Practices.'

'I thought you looked like a TWERP!' Boom! Boom! Even the cat enjoyed that one.

But then things took a turn for the worse: Dough rumbled my control panel plan. 'It's all very confusing, isn't it? One of those buttons may indeed bring my empire crashing down about my ears . . . But which one?'

I suddenly saw a large red button with an X on it. As Dough took out a revolver, I lunged and hit the button with my nose. That move could have made me a legend in my own lunge time! But instead of the hoped for cataclysm, the message 'Fooled You!' appeared on screens all around the gantry. Dash!

'You will perhaps forgive my little joke, Mister Brush. But now I'm getting tired of this charade.' He levelled his gun at me. My past life flashed before my eyes. It was rather interesting, actually – particularly lately. I'd never met the likes of Mister 'M', Mister 'Q' and so on before. I felt the comb Mister 'Q' had given me in my pocket. It was at that moment that I suddenly had a brilliant idea! I drew a bead on Doctor Dough and let him have . . . The Eye Of The Fox!

'Sneezing won't save you!' he barked. I really must revise my 'Eye' technique. 'It's goodbye, Mister Brush.'

Just then, the comb went off in my pocket, firing one of its teeth slap into Doctor Dough's right foot. Yes, those teeth must have been feet-seeking missiles! He doubled up in agony, dropping the cat and the gun in that order. 'Curse you,' he hissed. 'But the system is fully automated. Once I pull this lever—' Before I could get to him, he pulled the lever that set the entire operation into pouring, mixing, cooking, slicing and packing mode. He continued, '—the operation cannot be stopped except by deploying – as you guessed – the self-destruct button. But you will never find *that* in a million —'

Another of the teeth fired out of the comb – the bloomin' thing was uncontrollable – and made a bee line for the hot drinks vending machine at the far end of the gantry. It hit the 'white no sugar' button square on. The Doctor let out a yell as an almighty explosion lifted the roof off the cavern and shot thousands of tons of dough – alas in all its forms – hundreds of feet into the air. Moments later, the mixture was raining down like molten lava on the sea all around the island. Afterwards, the area looked rather attractive – like a sort of giant Victoria sponge!

And the power station? Fortunately, it was undamaged. And me? In bending down to rescue Dough's miserable moggy (successfully) I must have entered a natural air pocket that saved me from the blast. But for that dopey-looking puss, I might not be here today to tell the tale!

The subsequent party at Mister Noël's was a great success. All my new friends were there – including Mister Sid who was quite giddy with excitement, at one point uttering a complete sentence.

Mister Noël was generous in his praise for my efforts as 008 and I think he looked at me in a different light after what had happened. 'Basil, you achieved the impossible. How on earth did you do it?'

'Piece of cake!' Ha! Ha! Boom! Boom!

☆ ☆ ☆ ☆ ☆ ☆ ☆ ☆ ☆ ☆ ☆ ☆ ☆ ☆

CHAPTER SEVEN
ALL ABOUT FRED

☆ ☆ ☆

'These our actors,
As I foretold you, were all spirits and
Are melted into air. . .
We are such stuff
As dreams are made on, and our little life
Is rounded with a sleep.'
The Tempest, Act IV Scene 1

'Actors are like burglars – we work better at night.'
Anonymous

Despite my growing success on national television, I was still living in Bloomsbury with the Foxes. Much as we'd enjoyed our bachelor pad, we all felt it was time to move on. Edward and James were both doing very well and had even made some films – a medium that I was keen to exploit in the future. As for me, there were a number of reasons to transfer from Bloomsbury; not that the British

Museum had ever lost its charm, but I felt that there were more exciting parts of London for a young fox about town. Also, Edward and James were always asking about my trip to Jamaica which of course I had to keep mum about. Well, Queen Mum actually. Ha! Ha!

I took out a mortgage (another little something Harry Burns arranged) on a small studio flat in Notting Hill Gate – a 'happening' part of London and very convenient for Television Centre where I was to be seen most days, arguing with commissionaires, lunching with producers and chatting about football with Jimmy Hill. I was a keen Leicester City supporter as a cub and had even been given a trial – sadly only as a mascot. Unfortunately, my cousin Filbert got the job and as far as I know he's been there ever since.

But the main reason to move was the fact that we were all subjected to rather more regular visits from the family than we really wanted. Although it was lovely to see Mum and Dad and some of my siblings, it seemed that the allure of show business also attracted the attention of members of the family who one might otherwise have lost contact with. This is particularly true when you are part of a clan as extended as mine. Virtually every day would bring another phone call, letter or knock on the door from some distant aunt, uncle or cousin who happened to be in town and thought they would look us up. Especially me, as Edward and James always seemed to be in Hollywood, New York or Lowestoft at these times. Most departed quite happily after a cup of tea and a Rich Tea biscuit but some of them I would not be able to get rid of so easily, mainly because I could see they had nowhere to go and were looking for work. There was a couple who stayed with me for ages as roadies – I could see why they were referred to as yearlings because that was about the length of time they slept on our floor. Another cousin was the official photographer for my television shows, until it was discovered he was selling the pictures secretly to the newspapers and pocketing the money. This was also the time that I recorded my first record album and Deidre, my third cousin once removed, worked as one of the recording engineers.

The record, imaginatively entitled 'Boom! Boom! It's Basil Brush', included a monologue and a number of original songs penned by an old mate of mine, George Martin, who'd helped me write some of my television material. I don't think the sales were exactly astronomical although I know that it found a vinyl resting place in some of the hearts and most of the homes of my fans. Ha! Ha!

One of the tracks on the record was a number entitled, 'Basil the Bard' and reflected my love of Shakespeare. I thought that if I was going to be taken seriously as a comedy performer, I really ought to master the art of acting. Besides which the acting bug, which had lain dormant since my appearance at the Old Vic, had now infected my whole body. I wanted more. Due to my television commitments I didn't have time to attend a legitimate drama school, but I did find the time to attend the odd acting class.

Thus it was on a fateful Monday between television rehearsals that I found myself in a run-down rehearsal room just off the Strand with a group of would-be thespians. One chap in particular made a beeline for me during that first class, introducing himself as another student of the arts – one Fred Baxter.

Fred was quite extraordinary. I was immediately struck by his vulpine good looks, charisma and intelligence. He was just like me. In fact, he was so like me we could have been twins. I thought perhaps he was a long lost brother my mum had never told me about. We were roughly the same age, came from the same sort of background and he also possessed a similar sartorial elegance.

Although he was currently 'between engagements' and was working in that time-honoured actor's role as a waiter, Fred had taken on the mantle of 'actor laddie'. He referred to nearly everyone as 'darling heart' and those that he wasn't so keen on as merely 'darling'. I was quite taken with him, especially when he admitted that he had seen every television show I'd ever done.

Fred spoke adoringly of the noble art of acting. 'Wherever there's magic and make-believe and an audience there's theatre.' I would have loved to have heard more from him but unfortunately the teacher, a Liverpudlian called Eddie with an impenetrable scouse accent, began the class with an introductory exercise so that we could all get to know each other.

We had to play at being an animal of our choice, adopting their movements and sounds, portraying their character and finding the inner nature of the beast. Of course to you, dear reader, this may sound easy – but it certainly wasn't. Uncovering the essence of the animal, its reason for existence, innermost feelings and its motivation in an improvisational performance was quite a challenge. Anyhow, Fred and I decided, after much discussion, to be foxes. We set about our parts with vigour, enthusiasm and no little skill. We may perhaps have taken the 'method' approach a little too much to heart, judging by the terrified clucking of the young actress who had rather trustingly decided to be a chicken. Still, it didn't matter too much because her primeval screeching was lost amidst the cacophony of baying, howling and caterwauling that filled the room. Some bright spark had opted to be some sort of grumpy South American camel but the suggestion was greeted by the other students with some concern. I agreed and soon put an end to that. I said that there was no cause for a llama. Ha! Ha!

Although we enjoyed ourselves greatly, Fred and I did question the validity of such an exercise. By the time we'd also been asked to be 'a rockery', a 'garden shed' and a 'lawnmower', in what Eddie referred to as his 'landscape pathway to acting success', Fred was pretty fed up.

'It's ridiculous . . . all this talk about, "what I'm really looking for", searching for the "subtext", "the underlying meaning". Why can't we just try acting? No, I don't think he's very good and what's more I don't like him. I would say, a day away from him would be like a month in the country. Yes . . . he'd make a perfect stranger.'

Eddie implored us yet again to reach within ourselves and find 'the real us' but I'm afraid that the rockery business hadn't endeared Eddie to either of us – especially Fred. 'There is absolutely nothing in his background or his breeding that could have brought him closer to the stage than a seat in the upper circle.'

For a dog fox, Fred could be pretty bitchy.

Mind you, I did learn much more from Fred than Eddie. One thing he told me was that instead of spending hours learning lines you should write them on your cuffs, hands, a prop or even the stage set. It was much more useful advice than learning how to be a tree, something I didn't fancy much, especially if there was a dog in the cast which there seemed to be more and more in those days. Fred also had a wealth of theatrical stories, although his own experience was somewhat limited.

'I once appeared in a show at the Playhouse, Budleigh Salterton – how off Broadway can you get? A production of Agatha Christie's *Mousetrap*. Unfortunately the director – at least that's what he called himself – put live ammunition in a revolver and half the cast died in a hail of bullets.'

I looked suitably shocked but Fred continued breezily, 'Then there was a historical drama in which I played a courtier. The actor who was in the lead was so diabolical, one critic said, 'He played the king under the impression that someone else was going to play an ace.'

'It sounds like you've done a bit then,' I said tactfully.

'A bit, but I haven't had much luck so far. I was a patient in *Emergency Ward Ten* – half a dozen lines and then I went into a coma and never regained consciousness. Then there was another whodunnit, *Who killed Gregory Wainwright?* Guess who played Gregory Wainwright? I have been in films – well one. You must have seen *Zulu*. I was the first casualty. I caught a spear right in my opening sequence.'

I winced. 'Nasty.'

At the end of the class Fred approached me. 'Look, it's been absolutely marvellous working with you – why don't we do lunch sometime soon?'

And that was it really: the beginning of a friendship that didn't turn out to be exactly beautiful. We met regularly over the next few weeks, although not at the acting class as Fred convinced me that I was a natural and had little to learn. I wasn't entirely convinced but I was flattered just the same.

Sometime during this period, I suggested that he come and spend some time with me at the studios. He jumped at the idea with surprising enthusiasm and walked around the studios behind me as wide-eyed with wonderment as a star-struck ten year old, which also surprised me. He arrived wearing similar clothes to me and I noticed a number of people doing double takes when they saw us together. He was charming to everyone on the set and obviously loved being backstage. In the dressing room afterwards Fred was waxing lyrical and seemed genuinely moved to be involved. 'I love this business, you can breathe it can't you? That's some magic perfume.' I was delighted that he seemed to be enjoying the experience so much.

It wasn't long before Fred was spending more and more time at Television Centre – he was there almost every day. Once, coming back to the dressing room after a lengthy bout of rehearsing and filming, I found him in the company of Ursula, a young lady from the props department, doing impressions of yours truly. I mean Fred was doing the impression not Ursula – although she did actually do a very good Phil Silvers after a cocktail or two. I have to admit I was quite impressed with the accuracy of Fred's mimicry although I must have a looked a bit put out because once Ursula had left and the two of us were on our own, there was an awkward silence. After I'd changed into my civvies, he finally spoke: 'Darling heart, would you mind if I gave you a bit of advice?'

'Not at all,' I replied. I was getting rather used to Fred's advice.

'I think you work too hard,' he said. 'It's not good for you, you know. You're not as young as you were. Why don't you allow some of your fellow artistes to take the strain.'

I didn't disagree with him – apart from the crack about my age. Although I loved my work beyond anything, I was pushing myself hard and would often be up till two or three in the morning writing scripts, and then spend the whole of the following day rehearsing and filming.

'I mean,' he continued, 'do you really need to attend every rehearsal? You must know the lines, you wrote most of them after all.'

'I have to be there for the others. They need to see where I would be so they can react to me.'

'What if somebody very like you took over during read throughs and some rehearsals? You could rest and come to the performances fresh. I'm told that's what Dean Martin does. While the others are rehearsing he's out on a golf course somewhere. He watches tapes of the run-through and then turns up for the final recording.'

'I'd need to find someone I could trust,' I said and, as the words left my mouth, I realized what was coming next.

Fred spread his paws wide in a gesture that told me I had just summed up his thoughts exactly.

'As you know, dear boy, I'm resting at the moment. While I'm waiting for something to come up, let me do it. Let me be your understudy.'

I tried to persuade him to let me think about it, but he didn't leave me alone for a moment until I'd agreed, constantly telling me how tired I looked and how worried he was for me.

As it happened his timing was impeccable. Rodney

Bewes had just handed in his notice, wanting to get back to the acting thing and away from light entertainment. I tried to persuade him to stay but his mind was made up and eventually I had to admit defeat and allow him to go. We had replaced him with a young actor called Derek Fowlds, a delightful chap; I could see he had a natural talent for comedy and he also possessed a lovely selection of pullovers. As Derek grew into the role, I felt able to have Fred stand in for me in the less vital rehearsals. At the beginning, the arrangement worked very well and no one had any objections to this plan, which did indeed help me recoup some of my old energy.

As I had helped him professionally, Fred also started to confide in me about his personal life: 'I come from a very happy den – mum, dad, twenty-five siblings. The usual sort of thing. Both my parents worked: my father was a church minister in the Highlands and Islands of Scotland. Everyone loved him although I'm afraid he liked his tipple a bit too much and so his work suffered.'

'Don't tell me, he couldn't always find his way to the aisles. Boom! Boom!'

'My mother was a doctor in private practice.'

'I bet she was grateful for small fevers,' I quipped.

'Actually, darling heart, she was a surgeon.'

'I expect she was always working her fingers to the bone. Ha! Ha! Now, tell me about your brothers and sisters.'

'Oh, one of my brothers is really dim. You know what? When he's ill he jumps up and down before he takes his medicine.'

'Ah, that's because it says on the label, "Shake well before using".'

Fred was a great audience and loved feeding me the

lines. He guffawed uproariously and funnily enough I noticed that his laugh sounded just like mine. He started to say 'yes, yes, yes, yes' a lot in the same way that I had developed working with Mr Derek. I later realized that, although he was acting as a straight man, he was actually rehearsing a comedy routine and using me as a source of material.

It was soon after that he actually started to do the jokes: 'Have you ever wondered why sour cream has an expiry date?' 'When I left school and before I became an actor, I went travelling. It was a bit of a disaster – I caught yellow fever. Still, that was a long time ago – I'm definitely not feeling off colour now.' 'And another thing, if carrots are so good for the eyesight, how come I see so many dead rabbits on the roads?'

I laughed, of course, out of professional courtesy, but something in the back of my mind was worrying me. His delivery needed polishing, his material had no continuity, but I was mainly concerned that Fred had now become completely lost in his own world and I was his only source of reference.

Even then he seldom asked how I was and a glazed look would come over his face when the conversation wandered away from his favourite subject – him. He always seemed to be in my studio at Television Centre and when he started using my catchphrase, 'Boom! Boom!' in normal conversation, I began to wonder what he was up to. One day, he came to me and said that he'd been thrown out of his digs – not everyone had a sympathetic Mrs Crabtree to fall back on – and asked whether he could 'crash at my pad.' After a few minutes of fruitless discussion – mainly about Cape Canaveral – I finally worked out what he meant and I reluctantly agreed to take him in. No matter how annoying Fred had become, I couldn't bear to see him out on the streets. In those days, *The Big Issue* wasn't published so I don't know what he would have done to occupy himself on cold winter mornings.

Fred had only been in my flat for a week when I discovered that he'd been eating all my jelly babies, using my phone to contact his relatives and he'd even helped himself to selections from my joke book. He then told me that he hadn't realized what a ridiculously busy life I led and suggested becoming my personal secretary. This time I refused. I wanted to have some control over my life.

Of course, sharing a flat with me meant Fred soon picked up even more of my mannerisms, habits and rituals. His behaviour was beginning to scare me and I suppose I should have comprehended that something was awry when Fred signed up with a celebrity doubles agency. In a moment of quiet reflection I started to write the lyrics of a song that I was going to call, 'Send In The Clones'. I never did finish it – but it's an idea I might go back to sometime in the future.

Then some very strange things started to happen. I'd got into the habit of taking a nap on the afternoon of the television recording so that I would be in tip-top form for my evening's performance. I had never been late for important rehearsals – or any other professional engage-ment for that matter – in my life, but for several weeks in a row my alarm clock failed to go off. Each time I got to the studio – nearly an hour late – I found Fred about to record the show with Mister Derek.

At the studio, a microphone fell from the ceiling – and it was only the floor manager shouting 'Boom! Boom!' that saved me. Electric cables would rear up like vipers and come hurtling towards my throat. Television Centre's studio twelve had turned into a death trap. Amazingly Fred was always first on hand, checking that I was okay and suggesting I take the evening off and let him take my place in the recording. At first I thought that he was being incredibly thoughtful, but I knew in my heart of hearts that something wasn't quite right.

With new safety measures in place at the studio things calmed down for a while. And then the accidents started at home. A banana skin appeared for no reason at the top of the staircase, the hot and cold bath taps were mysteriously switched and the corners of my rugs always seemed to curl up dangerously. I noticed a funny glint in his eye when Fred wished me to 'break a leg'. He knew very well that this piece of theatrical folklore was only usually expressed when going on stage, and I couldn't quite understand why he was saying it to me as I was eating my cornflakes.

Then one fateful night I woke up to find Fred leaning over my bed with a hammer. He said he was checking to see if I needed any late night emergency picture hanging. After he'd gone, I didn't dare go to sleep for fear of what might happen and sat up all night long, clutching a copy of *Spotlight* for protection (volume three, female leading actresses, of course).

I was determined to discover if my terrible suspicions were true. The next evening I came home unexpectedly from work, tiptoed into the flat and found Fred slipping cyanide into my cream soda. I always like to think the best of people but I really felt that I had to say something this time. 'Fred, I know what you're up to. It won't work.'

'I thought you'd be—' he stuttered.

'I don't drink cream soda any more because I find I get the same effect by standing up really fast.' It was a bluff, of course, but I thought it might just work.

'Basil, darling heart, I thought you might be home early and so I was just . . . um . . .'

'I know what you're up to, Fred.'

'What do you mean?'

'You don't need to do this, you know.'

'Do what?' Fred was looking extremely uncomfortable.

I gave Fred 'The Eye Of The Fox'. 'It's over, Fred. Give it up.'

Fred looked back at me imploringly but he knew he was beaten. 'Basil, love, it's nothing personal, I didn't want to harm you – it's just this business – it gets hold of you and sometimes nothing else matters. All those things I told you about my background were untrue. I had a very unhappy upbringing. We had no money. There was no love in the family. Acting and make-believe began to take over my life – so much so that soon I couldn't tell the reality from the fiction.'

Show business, it's a fickle business. One day you're a star – the next an understudy. It could have been me standing there in his shoes. I was sympathetic. I then noticed he was actually standing there in *my* shoes.

'I suggest you go to ground for a while, Fred.'

'But Basil, I can't.'

'I promise not to say anything. Just leave now.'

A tear glistened in Fred's eye. 'Thanks, Basil. You're the best.'

'You've always been very quick to give me advice, Fred, now here's a little something for you: when you get off the track, lose your way, but then discover the right path, take the correct turn at the crossroads, hit the road to success and finally find yourself on that glittering showbiz highway, make sure of one thing.'

'What's that?'

'Fasten your seatbelt because it's going to be a bumpy night.'

With that I flounced out of the room and slammed the front door behind me. It was only when I reached Portobello Road that I remembered it was my flat and so I went home.

☆ ☆ ☆ ☆ ☆ ☆ ☆ ☆ ☆ ☆ ☆ ☆ ☆ ☆

CHAPTER EIGHT

THE SHOWS MUST GO ON

☆ ☆ ☆

'One reason people go into show business is so that they can sleep late. I know an act who was forty-five years old before he tasted cornflakes.'

Harry Burns, agent to the stars (and Jim Davidson)

Opening music.
Cartoon intro.
Fade up.
Camera pulls back to reveal Basil and Derek Fowlds by a river bank.
They are fishing.

DEREK Hello, hello, and welcome to the show.
BASIL (*singing*) Hello, hello, and to the show – welcome.
  Boom! Boom! Ha! Ha! Ha!

DEREK You know, Basil, it's lucky that we don't have wives, I don't think they'd approve of us spending so much time fishing. Especially if we lived in the Orient.

BASIL Do you mean Leyton Orient?

DEREK (*resigned*) In the East.

BASIL Oh, then you do mean Leyton. Ha! Ha!

DEREK (*patient*) What I mean is in the East, a man can have many wives. That's called polygamy. In Great Britain a man can have only one wife.

BASIL That's called monotony. Ha! Ha! Boom! Boom!

DEREK Have you had any luck with the fishing today?

BASIL Luck? Luck! It's not a matter of luck. It's a battle of wills. Pitting your wits against those of your prey. A cunning battle that draws on all your strength, intellect and ability.

DEREK So, have you caught anything?

BASIL No, I've been a bit unlucky. Ha! Ha!

DEREK Yes, well, fishing is a very popular hobby. It can just take hold of you and can easily become an obsession.

BASIL I know. Sometimes I think of it morning, noon and night. Last night I even had a terrible nightmare. I'd actually got this lovely big fish on the end of my line.

DEREK And then what happened?

BASIL It got away. I must have 'Dreamed the Impossible Bream'. Boom! Boom!

DEREK Don't point that pun at me – it could go off.

BASIL Hey, I do the funnies. Do you know what swims in the sea, carries a machine-gun and makes you an offer you can't refuse?

DEREK No.

BASIL The Codfather. Ha! Ha! Ha!

DEREK Oh dear. (*Pause*) Look, why don't we try
another part of the riverbank?

BASIL No. Anyway, it's no good – I'm going to have to
give up fishing – I can't stand to see the worms
drown.

DEREK Especially Willy.

BASIL Especially Willy.

DEREK How's he doing down there?

BASIL Oh, I don't use Willy any more. I've got a new
worm, George. He's luminous, so I can go fishing at
night.

DEREK That must be useful.

BASIL Yes, except sometimes he lights up when he
doesn't mean to. He can't always control himself.
You see, when you've got to glow – you've got to
glow. Boom! Boom!

DEREK It's no wonder you're a good swimmer –
you've been up the creek for years.

BASIL There's no point in trying to annoy me. I just
won't take the bait. The bait! Ha! Ha! Ha!

DEREK You know, I really don't think we're going to
catch anything here. We should have gone out in a
boat on the sea, like last time.

BASIL Yes, yes, yes. We could go back to the place
where we caught that plaice – or was it the plaice
where we caught that place?

DEREK Good idea. Didn't we mark the spot?

BASIL Of course! I put an 'X' on the side of the boat.
But it might not help us.

DEREK Why not?

BASIL Because, you twit, we might not get the same
     boat as last time! Ha! Ha! Ha!
DEREK They say that a fishing rod is a stick with a
     hook at one end and a fool at the other.
BASIL Watch it! A fool – what a cheek. Well, I bet you
     didn't know this: what do you get if you cross a whale
     with a computer? Give up? A four ton 'know it all'.
     Boom! Boom!
DEREK Boom Boom? What are you talking about?
     We're not in the boat now.
BASIL I told you – no jokes.
DEREK But I tell you who was in a boat. A pirate boat.
     That famous buccaneer Basil Redbeard. Did I ever
     tell you about the time. . . ?
Fade down.

I thought you'd enjoy that – an extract from an actual
script that we nearly recorded in the 1970s. The era that I
consider to be my golden age on television. Still that was a
long time ago and I've moved on. Sort of in one era and
out the other. Ha! Ha!

My career continued to soar through the seventies,
although there had to be a number of changes in the
straight men I worked with. Mister Derek decided he had
done long enough with me in 1973 and wanted to go back
to acting. I thought it was an awful shame since we'd got
to know each other well and worked so well as a team.

Derek and I had a lot of fun doing the show and apart
from the comedy in the script, I used to love slipping in an
ad-lib designed to give him a fit of the giggles or make him
'corpse' as we say. During a sketch once, I said, 'Did you

know that Mister Derek 'Fowldes' his money in two? That way he thinks he's got twice as much.' Derek fell about and then I turned to the audience and said, 'Derek's father is a man of letters – he works for the post office.'

Sometimes we had a bit of trouble with our guests. They'd often spend too long in the hospitality room before the show. One chap, in particular, came on the show at least five over the eight. I should have known that he would be trouble because he was a notorious boozer – but he had convinced us that he wasn't drinking any more. The trouble was, he wasn't drinking any less. Ha! Ha! We didn't pay him in the end – we just gave him some of Oliver Reed's empties to take back to the off licence.

What foxes me – sorry I'll rephrase that – what baffles me is how they managed to get worse for wear on BBC hospitality which usually consisted of a glass of house wine which has been compared to the Centre Court at Wimbledon – it's always well watered. Ha! Ha!

As for me, it was a glass of cream soda in the canteen. Now there are a lot of jokes about BBC canteens but I was quite happy to eat there. There was always a good atmosphere and usually some star or other would join you at the table. I remember once Benny Hill, that master of the single entendre, sat down with me. He was particularly wicked about his peers and finally I said, 'Benny, one thing we mustn't do is gossip about the butter knives – you know how those things spread.' Ha! Ha! That gag turned up in his next show! Typical Benny. No wonder he was nicknamed 'The Thief of Bad-gags.'

After the show, Mister Derek and I would usually go out to eat at our favourite little trattoria. The staff all knew us and helped us unwind. The proprietor, Luigi, always had the latest *Godfather* joke. My favourite was, 'What do you get when you cross the Godfather with a philosopher? An offer you can't understand.' Ha! Ha! Happy, halcyon days.

I was very fond of Mister Derek and about seven years after we parted I was delighted to see he'd got a part in a cult comedy series called *Yes, Minister*. It wasn't at all bad and revived his career for a good few years.

Harry managed to replace him with Mister Roy, a cheerful toothsome lad from Hull with a haircut like a member of Herman's Hermits. He lasted four years as well before deciding to go on to pastures new. He did a bit of presenting on children's television and then, I believe, he started touring all over England with various Shakespeare plays. You can just imagine some of the productions: *Much Ado About Worthing, The Comedy of Erith, A Midsommer Norton's Dream* and *The Two Gentlemen Of Ventnor*. Ha! Ha!

By the time he left me in 1977 my show was one of the mainstays of the Saturday night schedules on BBC1. My voice was as familiar to the public as Cilla Black's is today. Harry had managed to persuade Mister Howard to join us for a year. We had worked together before, when the show was still in its embryo stages but he'd gone off to make programmes about politics and economics. All that seriousness must have been getting him down because he jumped at the chance of getting back together with me for a couple of years of light relief. He then went on to form his own film company and I believe he now provides media training for diplomats.

I would have loved to have met up with him again and talked about the old times and also my work for the Foreign Office. I'm afraid to say that I did rather exploit these adventures to my advantage in other situations. You see, spying tales were always a great success with the ladies. It's no coincidence that James Bond has such an undying appeal with the opposite gender. They love a man who can use his brain as well as his brawn to get himself out of sticky situations. I found that telling the girls backstage that I worked for MI6 would nearly always gain me some advantage.

And, since this is a frank and full account of my life and times, and since you've been kind enough to shell out good money to peek behind my net curtains, I don't mind telling you I've always been particularly susceptible to being tickled behind the ears by a well-manicured finger or two. A girl who knows how to find the right spot can have my back leg thumping in uncontrollable pleasure.

And talking of 'leg thumpers', I feel I must mention my pet beagle, Ticker. I bought him at Battersea Dogs Home. I'd seen the notice, 'Buy one – get one flea'. He looked a sorry sight, I can tell you. Rather bedraggled, slobbering everywhere and with a terrible hacking cough. Apparently he had escaped from an animal research laboratory and had a 40 cigarette a day habit. (To my credit, I did manage to get him off the fags in the months to come by threatening him with Patches. Patches was the name of my neighbour's Alsatian.) Of course, it wasn't long before Ticker wanted to get into the act and pleaded with me – in a voice that sounded remarkably like Clement Freud's – to give him a break into show business.

I told him he was a silly pleader but I finally yielded to his demands. It seemed that everyone was trying to get into my act and most of them succeeded. I allowed him to walk and bark occasionally but not do too much else. He was happy with this arrangement and behaved himself, most of the time.

Meanwhile Mister Howard was duly replaced by Mister Billy, an Irish actor-singer who'd been appearing in the West End and was looking for a way to break through into the big time. He was later cast as an ex-boyfriend of Pauline Fowler's in *EastEnders*, which gave him a taste of the sort of fame which I'm sure all these young lads were hoping for when they teamed up with me.

Although I always felt sad when they went off and left me, I can understand why they did it. Show business is a cruel, fox-eat-fox world. It must have been hard for them, always being in my shadow, always being known as the chaps 'who worked with Basil Brush'. Maybe if I had been in their shoes I would have done the same. I certainly wouldn't have wanted to spend my whole career being Spike McPike's straight man.

Of course I was also doing all sorts of other things in those days – I appeared in a pantomime, *Babes in the Wood*, at the Beck theatre with Pete Murray and Chris Tarrant. I'm afraid my first walk on was rather spectacular – I was so busy bowing and playing to the audience, I wasn't watching where I was going and I bumped into a large tree in the middle of the stage. That crashed into the castle, which knocked the whole forest down. It wasn't exactly what I had been hoping for – although I suppose you could say I brought the house down. Ha! Ha!

Chris Tarrant was a lovely chap, although he was going through a bit of a turbulent time in his love life. Still, he had lots of pals and I suggested he contact one of them. 'Phone a friend,' I said. He must have got over it because he's been happily married for years and I see he's on television quite lot these days.

I also did lots of charity appearances and some of those naval chaps on board the Royal Survey vessel, H.M.S *Fox*, used me as a mascot and actually had an effigy of me on the quarterdeck. Those sailors are quite something. I must say some of them really fancy themselves – especially the officers. I knew of a captain who was so vain he said that he had joined the navy so that the world could see *him*. Ha! Ha!

I sometimes wish I'd kept a detailed diary during that period, like Tony Benn, Alan Clark, Adrian Mole and that Edwardian woman. All those power lunches with legendary show business figures would have fetched a tidy sum from the newspapers during some of the leaner times.

Having said that my diary entries in the early 1980s would not have been very interesting:

Monday   Woke up. Must ring Harry Burns.
Tuesday   Rang Harry Burns – not there – left a
      message.
Wednesday Had a shower – no word from Harry
      Burns.
Thursday   Ate my porridge – rang Harry Burns –
      no reply.
Friday   Rang Harry Burns – line dead.

I now knew what Harry meant when he explained to me that he was 'a rare breed of agent' – he was now so rare, he was virtually extinct. Ha! Ha! I suppose I ought to tell you about Harry's most recent transformation. His 'hippy days' had become 'his happy days'. The kaftans and the headbands had long since been burnt. Harry was now a Gucci-suited, ponytailed, Filofax grasping, business executive. One of Maggie's boys.

Up until then, I'd always been happy to leave all money matters to my management and Harry had seemed to be doing rather well. The house in Cheyne Walk became two houses – the second had been added to provide some more office space so that Harry didn't have to make the tedious commute to and from Regent Street every day. Although he still had a number of stars like myself on his books, he seemed now to be providing business advice to a much wider clientele, including some Eastern European gentlemen with interests in Jersey and some newly rich Arab princes.

Harry had also invested, 'for our future', *my* capital in forestry projects around the world. Since my family has always had a great fondness for forests this appeared to be a very appropriate place to be squirreling the money away, if one couldn't buy a confectionery manufacturing installation that is. Occasionally, I had managed to sneak a peek at his portfolio. Not a pretty sight, I can tell you. Take 'Parasol and Palm Tree Properties' – sounds a bit shady, doesn't it? Ha! Ha!

And then he advised me to put some money into 'Zone Rockets'. What was this – Britain's space programme? A firework firm? It was later explained to me that I'd misheard. The money was going not into his 'Zone Rockets' but 'His Own Pockets'. But I should have realized long before then that something was amiss.

I hadn't heard from him in quite a while and was now really beginning to worry about my Mr Burns. It was time to take some action. I went to his old office but there was absolutely no evidence that 'Interplanetary Entertainments' had ever existed and another business had been set up on the premises. I decided to visit him at home. I went first to one house and then the other in Cheyne Walk. The doors were now padlocked and there was no sign of life.

It was as if there was a plague on both his houses.

My gorge, if I had one, was rising. If he'd gone away for a little while – a short break or talent spotting on a cruise as he'd done several times before – he could have just warned me. But, a month after Harry disappeared, it became obvious he hadn't just popped off for a bit of a holiday. One morning, I picked up a Sunday paper for my usual leisurely weekend read and there it was in black and white: Harry had run off to South America with loads of innocent people's money – including mine. I was shocked and horrified that he could do such a thing and sought comfort in a half pound bag of jelly babies. I couldn't believe it. And even now I'm not sure Harry actually meant to steal the money. It's possible he just forgot to pass it on. He always was terribly forgetful about practical things like that, forgetting whether or not he'd put a cheque in the post or where he'd parked the Rolls before going into a restaurant for dinner, or wandering out of restaurants after meals without calling for the bill. You know how easily that sort of thing can happen.

Still, I have to say I certainly wasn't wild about Harry.

Then, one day, there was a phone call. I rushed to answer it, hoping against hope that it was some news about Harry Burns but it wasn't – it was from a Clarence House. I'd never heard of him and was somewhat taken aback when I picked up the receiver and heard a woman's voice, 'Is that you, Basil?'

'Yes, who's speaking?'

'It's Elizabeth.'

For a moment I was thrown off-balance. Now, whom did I know called Elizabeth? Well, it was a long time ago in the village near my parents' den. I was a young dog and there was a vixen I knew by that name. I don't remember much about her except that she was incredibly naïve. And I do recall that once she fell into the village pond and told everyone she was three months stagnant. Ha! Ha!

But this was a much older voice. 'Elizabeth?'

'Yes,' she said firmly. 'The Queen Mother.'

Oh *that* Elizabeth, I thought to myself. 'How nice to hear from you.'

'Yes, I'm sure it is. Are you free to meet me tomorrow?'

'Does that mean you want me to fix another poker game?'

'Oh, it was fixed, was it?'

'No, Ma'am – otherwise you would have lost.'

'But I won, didn't I. And where's my money?'

'But I thought that business in Jamaica meant that . . .' I stammered.

'I think we need to talk. Take me to lunch at the Ivy.'

'The Ivy?'

'Yes. I'll see you at one o'clock. And make sure you get a good table. Preferably near a waiter.'

'But . . .'

The phone was put down. I slumped into the nearest chair. I didn't need these problems. Getting out of a top security holiday camp is one thing – but getting into the Ivy. Of course, I would have to be completely indiscreet and mention the identity of my luncheon partner to ensure a reservation. And what's more, I'd be expected to pay.

The Ivy is, perhaps, the most famous theatrical restaurant in town. It is where actors and other celebrities are seen to go, and, indeed, where they go to be seen. It has quite an unpretentious façade, a comfortable interior and the only 'flash' thing about it is the photographic bulbs of the paparazzi who congregate outside. That day, there were none, and in fact the narrow street had been cleared and 'coned' by the police in anticipation of the royal arrival. Inside, most of the tables were occupied by some of the most famous names in the world of film and theatre. Sadly, though, there was no one I knew well enough to touch for a fiver. What with Harry ripping me off and the Queen Mother obviously angling for her money, I certainly wouldn't be able to pay the lunch bill. It appeared I'd be poison to the Ivy!

I was punctual as ever and reminded myself before I was joined by the Q.M. that it was bad manners to break your bread and roll in your soup. Ha! Ha! A few minutes later, a gleaming black Jaguar pulled up outside the restaurant. I could tell that it was a royal car by the stickers on the back window – 'We love Sandringham, Balmoral and Windsor'. The chauffeur opened the back door and assisted the Queen Mother out of the car. There was much bowing and scraping, although I told her it really wasn't necessary. Before long we were seated, drinks were being served and the food had been ordered.

'Mr Brush, you're being very abstemious.'

'Ah yes, Ma'am. I like to leave room for pudding. You see I'm very fond of a crumble or a sponge. They don't call me the "Dessert Fox" for nothing. Ha! Ha!'

'Oh, I thought you might be on a diet.'

'Well then I'd have ordered dishes that would take my breadth away. Boom! Boom!'

'You look pale,' said the Queen Mother. 'Is it having to tell those jokes or are you unwell?'

I thought I would throw myself on her mercy straight-away. 'Actually, Ma'am, I'm really rather stressed.'

'Oh dear. And why is that?' she enquired.

'I have to say, I'm broke, bankrupt, bereft of boodle.'

'Yes, money can be a problem,' she agreed, gently fingering her diamond and sapphire encrusted bracelet. 'But, you know something, Basil, money can't buy happiness.'

'Maybe – but at least you can be miserable in comfort.'

'Well, a lot of my money goes in the name of good causes,' she said. 'For instance, every week I donate quite a lot of my savings to sick horses. Mind you, I don't realize they're sick until after the race has finished.' I didn't react. 'Not funny, Basil?'

'Yes, I'm sorry, it's just too near the knuckle for me. You see, my agent has run off with all my money.'

'Oh dear,' the Queen Mother said sympathetically. 'I thought he was only supposed to take 10 per cent. Look, I think it's time I put you out of your misery. It's been rather unfair to keep you in suspense like this. I'm afraid I've been teasing you about the poker debt.'

'What do you mean?'

'We were very pleased with how things went in Jamaica – so I am prepared to overlook the money you owe me.'

'Thank you,' I said greatly relieved.

'And, for the magnificent duties that you performed in

the service of your country, I wouldn't be surprised if, at some later date, you didn't receive a little accolade.'

My face fell. 'That's a bit much. Considering all I did, I think I deserve more than just a bottle of that fizzy orange energy drink.'

'Very good, Basil. It's nice to see you back on top form. And finally, you'd probably like to know that this lunch is on the house.'

'The House of Windsor?'

'Oh no, the Ivy. They never let me pay here. This will be on them. Whenever I'm about to be presented with the bill, I knock over my gin and tonic, make a terrible fuss of looking through my handbag, dropping my cigarettes and betting slips all over the floor. By the time I've recovered myself, they're too embarrassed to ask me to pay. You must try it sometime. Now, in light of what I've just said, perhaps you'd like another look at the menu?'

Lunch with the Queen Mother cheered me up no end, reminding me that a fox who can look annihilation in the face with a merry smile whilst outwitting a megalomaniac like Doctor Dough could certainly overcome the small matter of losing all his money. But quite what to do about my future required some thought and I decided there was only one place for me at a time like this. I had to go home.

Thus the prodigal son returned and was welcomed like a hero. Although I wasn't exactly feeling full of the joys of spring, I behaved like a true pro and put on my usual garrulous act. I laughed and joked with everyone as if I was on top of the world. It seemed as if I had successfully fooled the family. But, of course, I hadn't.

At lunch, the day after I came home and whilst Dad was at work, Mum and I were munching on some chicken sandwiches. 'I've been reading the papers,' she said, 'I know what's happened. Why didn't you tell me, Basil?'

'I didn't want to worry you.'

'Don't be silly, Basil, I'm your mother.' She squeezed my paw lovingly. 'We'll look after you for the time being. And, you know, in a funny way it's probably all for the best.'

'How do you mean?' I enquired, a little puzzled.

'Well,' she said with a thoughtful look on her face, 'you've been pottering along in the same way for years, doing your show for the BBC, living in the same little flat. I did wonder, darling, if it wasn't time for a new challenge. Perhaps a shake-up like this Harry Burns business is a sign that things were meant to change.'

She'd put into words exactly what I had been feeling. Mothers are amazing. 'I suppose I could go back on the road,' I said. 'I could arrange a national tour, maybe I could do a bit of straight acting as well – I've had some experience now. If that doesn't work out, I could do a *Carry On* film.'

'No!' she held up her hands to stem my babbling. 'That's not the way forward.'

'What is then?'

'You're going to Hollywood.'

'What?' I didn't have a clue what she was talking about.

'Look what happened to Dudley Moore,' she explained. 'He's become an international heartthrob. Just like you, he got fed up with the modern comedy scene over here, so he went . . . over there.'

Dudley Moore had just released a film called *Ten* in which he played a middle-aged man in love with a young

Bo Derek, pursuing her on her honeymoon and eventually managing to get into bed with her, with hilarious results. The world had gone mad for the film, partly because of Dudley's comic timing, partly because Bo Derek was a bit of a fox.

'He only got the part because George Segal dropped out,' I protested.

Mum was vehement. 'That's not why he got the part. He got the part because he was *there* when George Segal dropped out. You need to be in Hollywood, amongst the shakers and movers, shaking and moving with the best of them. Your dad thinks so too. You know he's always encouraged you to be adventurous and seek new frontiers – in all aspects of your life.'

'Dad knows about all this?' I asked. I was disappointed and yet relieved at the same time.

'Of course he does. And, just in case it took them a little while to "discover" you,' she paused for dramatic effect, 'we've got you a movie deal.'

Suddenly Mum had taken on the character of a Sam Goldwyn. I was both excited and intrigued. 'Go on.'

'Your Uncle Louis has just been made an executive at Twenty-First Century Fox. I've spoken to him and he's promised to help. He's seen your work and thinks you're wonderful. In fact, he said he's been thinking of a vehicle for you for a while and has lots of ideas.'

'Mum, I don't know what to say. You and Dad . . . you're just . . .' Words failed me – probably for the first time in my life.

We hugged each other and the tears ran down our cheeks, over our snouts and on to our chicken sandwiches. 'Mum, there is one thing I must ask.'

'Yes, Basil, what is it?'

'Could you look after Ticker while I'm gone? I couldn't bear to see him go back to Battersea.'

'Have a beagle in the den? I'm really not sure. You know what your father thinks of hounds.'

'I know – but Ticker's house-trained, he's got a lovely nature and he's given up smoking.'

'Well, that is a relief. Don't worry, Basil, I expect it will be all right. I'll have a quiet word with your father.'

'Thanks, Mum.'

I was suddenly scared about the future. 'Mum, do you think *I'll* be all right?'

'Basil,' Mum held me even tighter. 'You are the best. A shining light in the galaxy, just temporarily in the shadow. You're a true star. And you always will be. You are going to be a huge success in Hollywood where you will be adored and treated like the multi-talented celebrity that you are. But in the meantime, there is just one thing that I ask.'

'What's that, Mum?'

'Would you please do some washing up? I've got to phone Uncle Louis.'

CHAPTER NINE

HOLLYWOOD – A GREAT PLACE TO LIVE IF YOU'RE AN ORANGE

'This is not a tough job. You read a script. If you like the part and the money is okay, you do it. Then you remember your lines, you show up on time. You do what the director tells you to do. When you finish you rest and then go to the next part. That's it. But that's not how Basil did it. Basil, he was different. He lived his roles . . . He is Mr Method. I once said to him that he made Brando look like a dilettante . . . Basil seemed pleased.'

Louis Brush
President, Twenty-First Century Fox

A week later I stepped off a jumbo jet at Los Angeles airport or LAX as it's known locally. Apparently, it's known locally as LAX because . . . Oh no . . . it's much too early in the chapter for toilet humour. Now, where was I? Oh yes . . . I found myself standing in line (I'd already begun to pick up a working knowledge of the language from an English/American phrase book) at U.S. Immigration. After what seemed hours, it was finally my turn. I stepped across the yellow line on the floor and came face to face with my first real American. A stern young woman in a glass booth, sitting behind a computer.

'Hi, my name is Dolores and I'm your Immigration Officer for today.'

'Well, hello Dolly. Ha! Ha! It's so nice to see you . . .'

'What is the purpose of your visit?'

'To make people laugh. Ha! Ha!'

'Well, you've certainly succeeded with your clothes, sir.' Dolores didn't crack a smile as she checked the details of my passport and typed my details on the screen to verify that I wasn't a desperado on the run.

'Have you ever borne arms against the United States or indulged in any terrorist acts?'

'Well, I did get one review that described my act as a crime, but that's the closest I've come to terrorism.'

'Are you carrying any firearms?'

'No. Absolutely not – although I've got a rather useful Swiss army knife that can take stones out of horses' hooves.'

'How long are you staying?'

'Well, I'm hoping for a part in a film – so I would think at least six months depending on how the shooting goes . . .'

'Ah . . . you're an actor. Yeah, that's just what we need

in this town – another actor. I guess that explains that laugh of yours.'

'Ha . . .' I stopped myself just in time.

'So you're hoping to work whilst you're here?'

'Oh yes, I'm not workshy.'

'Okay, I'll give you a three month visitor's visa and if you seek work whilst you're here, you'll have to upgrade your status. Have a nice stay, sir. But do remember about your status.' She stamped the passport and smiled as she handed it back to me. I think she'd taken a shine to me.

'Thanks so much. I will.' I'd heard that they were status conscious in Los Angeles but this was ridiculous.

Customs wasn't quite so straightforward. I suspected things were starting to go wrong when they asked me if I had anything to declare and I remembered that old Oscar Wilde line, 'only my genius'. It was not the most original line and from the looks on their faces I could see I was not the first English entertainer to use it on them. Maybe the Boom! Boom! at the end also caused them some suspicion. Not sure whether I would be able to get them in America, I'd packed a six months' supply of jelly babies at the bottom of my bag. (I'd only brought boy jelly babies because I'd always found you got more for your money.)

I was rather startled, when the customs officials opened my case with almost no hint of civility, to find myself the centre of attention amongst a group of men wearing large guns on their hips. After much discussion they decided to confiscate my jelly babies – apparently you're not allowed to bring foodstuffs into the Sunshine State. Something to do with the Californian fruit fly. No amount of coaxing, cajoling or persuading would convince them that my sweets were not a threat to the entire

Californian agricultural industry and so I waved goodbye stoically to my babies.

I hurried through to the arrival gate and I was delighted to see, in the crowd of faces, someone who I presumed to be a representative from Twenty-First Century Fox. A young man with floppy blond hair sprouting from a black chauffeur's hat, wearing a rather colourful shirt covered in palm trees and an outsize pair of khaki shorts. He was thrusting a placard in the air which bore the hand-written slogan, 'Fox welcomes Basil Brush'.

'Hi, my name is Quinn and I'm your driver for the day.' He offered his hand in a somewhat odd manner and mentioned something about 'giving him five'. I thought that one handshake was quite enough as I hardly knew him and so I took my paw away rather sharpish.

Quinn grabbed my bag and led me through the airport until we reached the car. I'd never seen anything quite like it. A pink stretch limo that . . . well . . . seemed to stretch into Nevada. I presumed Uncle Louis had chosen this as a joke.

'You wanna ride up front? It's just that some of the guys I drive around aren't used to taking a backseat – even in a limousine like this.'

'No, I'm perfectly happy in the back – in fact I don't think I could even find the front of this car,' I said as I climbed into the rear of the limo and sank back into the luxurious black leather upholstery.

Quinn looked at me in his rear view mirror, 'I hear you're some kind of English hot shot entertainer. Well, if you think you're gonna make it in this town, I wish you luck, man.' He started the car, the engine purred into life and we were off. 'I've been here five years and nothing has happened in my career. And I was top of my class. Yeah, I'm an actor too.' Quinn was soon regaling me with his hard luck stories, lost opportunities, 'industry' corruption and a mixed combination of excuses about why he hadn't made it in Hollywood. 'I hate this town.'

'You should try Frinton.' I replied.

The car suddenly screeched to a halt and Quinn started to hoot, wave and shout. A glamorous woman in headscarf and sunglasses waved back. 'Did you see who that was?'

'No, I'm afraid I didn't recognize her.'

Quinn set off again. 'That was Meryl Streep. I love this town.'

'Does that happen a lot – seeing film stars on the street, like that?'

'All the time, man. Kind of strange, isn't it? It's like Fred Allen said, "A celebrity is a person who works hard all their life to become well known, then wears dark glasses to avoid being recognized." '

Whilst Quinn droned on about what Bette Davis had once said to Joan Crawford, Liz Taylor's latest husband and the story of Lana Turner being plucked from obscurity at Schwabs drug store, I looked out of the car window. My goodness, it was night already – time had flown. Then I realized the windows were tinted. I wound the window down. I still couldn't see much – this time it was due to 'the thermal inversion layer' that I had read about in all the guide books, or smog as it's more widely known. However, as we neared Beverly Hills, the weather had changed and the sun was now shining cats and dogs. Ha! Ha!

I could now clearly see the pale, tropical light, palm trees floating down sunkissed boulevards and the opulence of the neighbourhood; Beverly Hills, where the people are so rich, the kids put Perrier in their water pistols.

Quinn dropped me off at the salmon pink Beverly Hills Hotel, my home for the foreseeable future. The hotel and the shocking pink limo created a terrible colour clash, which the hotel staff must have spotted as they were quick to usher Quinn away. I wished him luck and he told me that he was going 'back east' for a while to get his 'head together.' He also remembered to tell me that Uncle Louis was going to meet me in the famous Polo Lounge for cocktails that evening.

I checked in at reception and was quickly and efficiently shown to my palatial suite by Diego. 'Hi, I'm your customer facilitator for the day.' The suite was incredible – almost as spacious as the back of the limo with a king size bed, television screen in the ceiling, jacuzzi (Diego had to point this feature out to me when I complained about the noisy plumbing) and a mini bar stocked with a seemingly endless supply of my favourite tipples. It was so posh there were bowls of fruit everywhere, and no one was even ill. Ha! Ha!

Before he left, Diego explained in a bored and monotonous voice, 'For your convenience today, we at the Beverly Hotel are pleased to have as guests the following: by the pool you will find Alan Alda and Jane Fonda. In our world famous Polo Lounge, Raquel Welch and her agent are discussing her next movie. Jack Nicholson is having a late breakfast with a selection of babes who have yet to be famous and Farrah will be floating throughout the hotel giving all the guests an opportunity to recognize her. If there is anything further you require, please talk to my agent. Goodbye.'

I was so exhausted with all the excitement, not to mention jet lag, I grabbed a quick nap. When I woke up, I realized that I'd just had a wonderful dream. I dreamed that the Joneses were trying to keep up with me. Boom! Boom!

I was about to go downstairs to meet Uncle Louis when I received a phone call. It was Joan Collins, of all people. 'Basil, darling,' she drawled down the line, 'I heard you were in town. We absolutely must have lunch tomorrow. Come to mine. We Brits have to stick together out here or they'll chew us up and spit us out.'

I've always been very fond of Joanie. We first met during the Sixties. After the success of her film *The Bitch*, which was based on one of her sister's books, her people had been thinking of making a sequel called *The Fox* and got in touch with me to see if I would be interested in co-starring and maybe helping with the writing. We talked a lot about the project and Joanie was very keen, but in the end Harry vetoed it, saying it might compromise my family appeal if I appeared in an X rated movie. So they changed the script and called it *The Stud* instead. Joanie had always said it wasn't half the film it could have been if they'd stuck to their original plan, which was sweet of her.

I wandered down to the Polo Lounge much encouraged by the call. This was getting exciting. I sat in the corner and ordered a cocktail from the waiter who asked if I wanted to 'run a tab'. I told him it was not necessary as I'd just taken a shower. I soaked up the glitzy show business atmosphere of the lounge. Agents and producers were pitching ideas, actors were bitching about each other and writers were pinching – mainly the free hors d'oeuvres. I suddenly heard this little voice in my ear,

'Mr Brush, you look very smart.' I looked around but there didn't seem to be anyone talking to me. I returned to my drink. 'Mr Brush, you really are very funny.' Still no one obviously trying to attract my attention. When I heard this voice for the third time, telling me how successful I was going to be in Hollywood, I caught the barman's eye and explained to him what had happened. He pointed in the direction of a bowl of olives on my table, 'Don't worry sir, it's the olives – they're complimentary.' Ha! Ha!

Then Uncle Louis arrived, looking much as I'd remembered him apart from the fact that he'd put on a bit of weight. He still smoked a cigar the size of a submarine.

'It's great to see you, Basil, you look terrific.'

'Thanks, Uncle Louis. This is a marvellous hotel.'

'I'm glad you like it here. Did you know that this hotel is renowned for its peace and solitude? In fact, people from all over the world flock here to enjoy its solitude.'

'Ha! Ha! How have you been, Uncle Louis?'

'Well, I've been doing pretty well since I last saw you. I'm in great health, the studio is successful and I have a fabulous house in Malibu.'

'And how's Aunt Gloria?'

'Ah,' Uncle Louis took a reflective puff of his cigar. 'She's history, I'm afraid, Basil. We're divorced. In fact I've been married several times since then.'

'Really?'

'Yeah. Shame you couldn't make any of the weddings. I always have the service in the morning.'

'That way – if it doesn't last, you haven't ruined the whole day.'

'Hey, that's my punchline, Basil.'

'And that's my joke,' I added.

'Yeah, right, I forgot who I was talking to.'

'It's great to be here, Uncle Louis.'

'It's great to have you here. Now look, Basil, this deal is not just because we're family. I've always loved your work and I think we can come up with something special here.'

'Thanks. I hope so.'

'Well, we're relying on you for a box office hit. The last movie we made was a real turkey. It was so bad even the popcorn got panned.'

'Don't tell me – the film wasn't released, it escaped.'

'Exactly, Basil. You're talking my language.'

Uncle Louis went on to outline some of his thoughts and ideas about how I was going to feature in the studio plans. After hearing all this and having knocked back a couple of Dream Cream Soda Sling Fizzes, I was feeling pretty good.

'What do you have in mind for me, Uncle Louis?'

'Listen, kid, I'm going to get you on the A list. But before you get too excited, let me give you some advice about Hollywood. Keep your paws on the ground and don't listen to any of the hype. All you really need to know is which part of the avocado to throw away. Do you understand what I'm saying?'

'Yes, I think so.' I was a bit baffled but still . . .

'Now let's have one more drink. Pass me that last olive.'

'Actually, Uncle Louis I'd like to keep it – as a souvenir.'

'Well, whatever, Basil. Soon you may be able to buy your own grove.'

The following day I went to the poolside lunch at Joan

Collins' house. There were a few other ex-pat Europeans like Michael Caine, who I had never met. He was very friendly and although he was somewhat disparaging about the tax system in England, he admitted to being a bit homesick. 'I get a bit fed up with all this sunshine, to be honest. It's funny what you miss – I thought I saw a robin the other day but realized it was just a sparrow with sunburn.'

Also in attendance was a young Austrian called Arnie who had been Mr Universe. He was a little hard to understand, having an accent as thick as the caviar in one of the sandwiches, but he seemed to be on much the same track as us, wanting to transfer his talents to the big screen and become a movie star. I remember feeling rather sorry for him, not seeing quite how he would fit in to the English-speaking scene, but I needn't have worried. Within a few years he'd pulled his English up far enough to become the biggest movie action hero on the face of the planet. He was a good-natured lad, keen to show off his torso at every opportunity, and I indulged him in a little arm-wrestling to make him feel less left out. I think he was surprised by my wiry strength.

It was at this gathering that I met the legendary Robert Mitchum. Joan and he had worked together (along with my old mucker, Edward Fox) on the remake of *The Big Sleep* and had stayed in close contact. 'Bob', as we in the movie world call him, had a blonde on each arm but he still found the time to be charming to me whilst they were fetching his drinks.

Joan was terribly excited about her latest project. 'Haven't you seen it? It's a sort of grand soap opera about very rich people,' she purred happily. 'It's called *Dynasty*.

135

It's the most fabulous part. I tell you, darling, television is so much fun. With a film you slave for months to produce something that goes in and out of the cinemas within a few weeks, with television you're appearing in people's homes, week after week after week for years, all over the world.'

'Who else is in it?'

'The lead is John Forsyth. He's just so gorgeous. But then look at you, Basil. You're quite a dish yourself.'

'Oh, how sweet of you, Joanie. But you're only saying that because it's true.'

'This is one hot fox,' she told everyone she introduced me to that day. Her friends all looked very important, with their designer clothes and haircuts, their dark glasses and their capped teeth, all terribly *American Gigolo*.

One hot fox . . . I liked the sound of that.

The Twenty-First Century Fox studios were situated in Santa Monica, just a few blocks from the pounding waves of the Pacific Ocean. Uncle Louis' office was on the top floor of a mini-skyscraper, a modern superstructure of glass and steel and with a vista to die for.

The meeting was larger than I'd expected with a number of energetic executives all trying to impress Uncle Louis who was, it transpired, actually the head of the studio.

'Gentlemen, meet Basil,' he said with an expansive wave of the cigar. My 'Good morning, chaps' was greeted by an outburst of enthusiastic plaudits: 'Great to have you on board', 'Nice piece in *Variety* about you', and the simple but evocative, 'You're wonderful, just wonderful.' These men were introduced by Uncle Louis as producers and the various heads of creative affairs. I wasn't sure whether this described their job descriptions or the state of their marital entanglements but judging by some of the banter, I think it was the latter: 'I remarried my wife, so I didn't have to pay alimony.' 'My wife used to be beautiful but she's let herself go. She used to turn heads but now she turns stomachs. I'm looking elsewhere, guys, I'm looking.' 'My second marriage broke up five minutes after the ceremony – I had to sue my wife for custody of the cake.'

Uncle Louis apologized to me on their behalf, 'Don't mind them, Basil, they're just being themselves this morning.'

I sat back and listened to the movie talk that followed, with silver screen terms such as 'treatments', 'concepts', 'box office hits', 'properties', 'bankrolling', 'sequels', 'prequels' and 'tax write offs' amongst many others. Most of it went over my head although my ears did prick up when they mentioned a budget of 15 million dollars. That would buy a few jelly babies.

Finally one of the execs, Irving I think was his name, turned to me, 'So, Basil, who do you want to work with?'

'Well, I've always liked . . .' I named a Hollywood veteran that I'd long admired.

'No, no, no. He's much too old. Anyway, we're looking for a female star.'

'Are we? Okay, how about . . . ?'

'What's the matter with you, Basil. Are you kidding? I went to her last birthday party. I'll never forget the cake – there were so many candles the ceiling got barbecued. Think younger!'

'Have you heard of Michelle Pfeiffer?'

'No.'

'That's a shame. Still, you will one day. Well, you must know Miss Goldie Hawn.'

Uncle Louis sprang to life. 'Great call, Basil. Hear that, Irving? Get Swifty on the line. See what you can do.' Uncle Louis seemed pleased with me. 'I like that, Basil. Now we need a concept. And please, don't anyone mention another civil war epic like the last one. Just whose idea was that musical, *Three Guys from Gettysburg*? This time let's pick a winner. Who's got what?'

The executives were falling over each other with suggestions. 'It should be a disaster picture. A fox saves a group of children trapped in a mineshaft that is filling with poisonous, flammable gases! *Poseidon Adventure* meets *Towering Inferno!*'

'What about a remake of *Bringing Up Baby*? Basil's perfect for the Cary Grant part. Goldie Hawn is the new Katharine Hepburn – only different. It could be big, big, big.'

And so the talk went on, and round, and back to where it started, with everyone chipping in their 'fabulous' ideas – sci-fi spectaculars, modern westerns, horror films, 'feelgood' movies. Everything, it seemed, was possible, but nothing was definite.

I decided that I'd sat there long enough taking this all in. It was time to spring into action, 'I know. Why don't we do a sort of sequel to *Foul Play*. A wacky . . . adventure . . . romantic. . . comedy.'

'That's terrific!' This from Uncle Louis. 'Tell me more, Basil.'

'Well, this is all off the top of my head but . . . let's see . . . yes . . . Miss Hawn can play the character of Gloria again – she's still the same sweet librarian. I'm a visiting

English private detective and we stumble on a group of criminals hell bent on blowing up a chicken farm. We could call it . . . oh I don't know . . . *Fowl Play*. As in F-O-W-L,' I stressed.

Uncle Louis was stunned. 'Steven, write this down. Go on, Basil.'

'Well, along the way, we come across lots of zany, comical, evil and mysterious characters probably with limps, scars and deformities. I play against type by empathizing with the chickens and Miss Hawn and I save the day – and then, well, I wouldn't be surprised if we don't just happen to fall in love.'

'Fabulous, fabulous, fabulous. Basil you're a genius. Okay. Now, who's going to write it?'

'Actually, I've always thought I was a rather good with a pen.' That stopped them in their tracks. 'I could show you my CV if you like,' I continued.

Uncle Louis slapped me heartily on my back, causing me to nearly choke on the toffee I had surreptitiously popped in to my mouth. 'We don't need to do that. I can vouch for you. Okay. We'll get our people to talk to your people.'

'I'm afraid I don't have any people. You see, I'm between agents.'

'This is even better news. Agents are the pits. You know the difference between an agent and a herd of elephants? The agent charges more. Boom! Boom! – if I can use your catchphrase?'

'Just this once, Uncle Louis.'

'Thanks Basil. You know, I think we might just have a picture.'

And that's how my Hollywood career began. I was

given an office on the studio lot and a team of writers were allocated to 'hone', 'revise' and 'sharpen' my screenplay. By the time I caught sight of the final draft, it was pretty unrecognizable. Still I could always use my original script for the sequel.

When I was a young fox I used to be a real cinema lover – I actually had a job as an usher in the local picture house. I described myself then as one of the cinema's leading lights. There was an usherette that I rather liked. In fact, I carried a torch for her for a while. Ha! Ha! The whole atmosphere of the cinema excited me. The curtains drawing open, the lights going down and all the familiar sounds like the rustle of sweet papers or the chomping of popcorn. I also enjoyed those film trailers, even though I couldn't help thinking – why does next week's film always look better than the one you've just seen? Adventure, romance, thrills – it was all up there on the screen and I used to fantasize that I was that hero. I was fighting the villains, chasing the crooks, crossing swords with the wicked Sheriff of Nottingham. I had the matinee idol looks, and the heroines always fell in love with me. It was a dream world I lived in. But now, amazingly, the dream had come true. Here I was, in the home of the movies, Hollywood. I was going to be a big star with my name above the title.

I'd have more money than I could shake a stick at, possibly an Oscar nomination. I was getting carried away and I hadn't even set foot on the set yet. But then that's the magic of Hollywood.

As I mentioned earlier, I have never kept a proper diary, but I did scribble a few notes I made about the first day of filming at the studios:

Crawled out of bed at 5.30 a.m., excited but weary. An hour later, I was at the studio. My trailer is comfortable. Name on the door. Lavatory. Jelly baby dispenser. It's still not quite the luxury condominium on wheels that Miss Hawn seems to occupy. But then she is a famous star – an Oscar on the mantelpiece (her trailer even had a mantelpiece) and a fair number of movies to her credit.

Meet Miss Hawn for the first time. Her first words to me are, 'Hi, Baz, it's a pleasure to meet you. I feel a good vibe.' She's funny, charming and delightfully enthusiastic. She admits that she hadn't heard of me when she got the script and wasn't sure whether or not to accept the part. I say something to her about 'the dilemmas of a Hawn'. She laughs. I admit to her that I was a little nervous. She gives me a hug. 'Don't worry, Baz, I can tell that we have a rapport already. Why don't you call me Goldie.'

First day's shooting was great. Working with Miss Goldie is a joy. An absolute delight.

We were now into the third week of production of *Fowl Play* and so far it had had been a most enjoyable experience. Everyone seemed to like the script and fortunately my performance had been greeted with universal praise. Portraying a private detective isn't as easy as it looks, you know. It's not given to everyone to be able to ask questions, jot down notes, nod intelligently every so often – all whilst wearing an unfamiliar hat – and not make a complete hash of it.

We had just finished shooting a scene which I thought had gone particularly well when something extraordinary happened. Before the director could make his way across, Miss Goldie came rushing over like a bunny on springs. Yes – it was another California Goldie rush! Ha! Ha!

'Basil, that was delicious! I'm hungry for more!'

'If you think *that* was delicious, you should have seen my *Hamlet* in Madrid. And when you're hungry there's nothing like a good old Spanish Hamlet! Boom! Boom!'

'You are *so* funny!'

'Could I have that in writing, please?'

Miss Goldie chuckled. That wonderful girlish giggle – just like she used to do so disarmingly in *Laugh In*, one of my favourite television shows. I must admit that I was becoming somewhat smitten with my co-star. And I was just about to ask her if she might fancy a cream soda after we 'wrapped' for the day – I wonder what they actually wrap? The cameras? – when without warning, the very ground seemed to shake beneath our feet and Miss Goldie launched herself uncontrollably into my arms. Mister Noël had once told me that there would be moments like this in my life so I knew what to say: 'My dear, did the earth move for you too?'

But before Miss Goldie could respond, there was a deep reverberating rumble – I knew I shouldn't have eaten that burrito – and a microphone mounted on a whacking great pole came crashing down loudly about our ears.

All around, lighting rigs were falling down, cameras were disappearing through gaping holes in the floor and people were sliding, tumbling and running amok all over the place. It was like panto season all over again! Finally, a gorilla dressed as a camel came flying through a gap in the wall from the adjoining studio – they were filming *The Desert Kong*! – and landed in a great billowing cloud of powder, slap bang on top of Miss Goldie's make-up artist. Talk about getting the hump! It was quite a sight, I can tell you. Personally, I don't think 'honey beige' is a good colour for a gorilla. It clashed with his eye shadow! Ha! Ha!

I suddenly noticed that Miss Goldie, who only seconds before had been nestling in my arms . . . was gone. After several moments of worryingly fruitless searching among the debris – although what use fruit would have been to me at that moment I don't know – the gorilla, who it turned out was called Nigel and hailed originally from Sittingbourne, tipped me the wink as to her whereabouts. And the direction of that wink tip was upwards.

'Are you all right, Miss Goldie?' I called out. 'I only ask because you seem to be in a spot of bother.'

'You call being suspended by my hot pants straps from a crane fifty feet in the air in the middle of an earthquake "a spot of bother"!?'

Then, just when I thought things couldn't get any worse – they did. The crane from which Miss Goldie was dangling decided to fly south for the winter – in one fell swoop! As the contraption broke up all around her, the hook which had caught on Miss 'Happy Hollywood's' hot pants suddenly jerked backwards, catapulting her through the air with a loud 'doyoyng' at what can only be described – brace yourselves dear readers – as 'break neck speed' towards the one section of wall that still remained in the place. Oh no! What to do?

At that precise moment, a huge ladder thrust up through a hole in the studio floor and landed at my feet. It gave me an idea. If some *one* or some *thing* of superhuman strength could only raise and steady it, I might be able to save Miss Goldie yet. In short, where was there a gorilla when you needed one? A gorilla! I looked back to where I'd last seen Nigel but he wasn't there. Dash! But then just as I was beginning to fear the worst, I suddenly caught sight of him pitching a screenplay idea to a producer who had become hopelessly snarled up in a tangle of sparking cables, wires and ropes at the far end of the studio. I could see that for some reason it wasn't going well but there was nothing for it – I had to interrupt. 'Nigel, grab this ladder and hold it up!'

As Nigel tried a new tack with the producer – 'Could you see it as a musical?' – he caught hold of the ladder and nonchalantly hoisted it skywards. Now for it! I scampered up, reached the top rung and launched myself into space, hoping that some trace of the flying fox branch of the family's expertise in such matters would come to my aid. It didn't. But I was still just in time to catch Miss Goldie before she shot past. She seemed comforted. 'Aaargghhh!' she screamed.

But she needn't have worried. The impact of my interception had knocked Miss Goldie slightly off her original trajectory and into a set of heavy drapes that were miraculously still hanging adjacent to the wall. We landed in them with no more than a floppy plop and then slid down them to safety as pleasantly as you like.

'Basil – I don't know if what you just did was the most foolish or the bravest thing that anyone has ever done. But I *do* know that it was the most incredible!'

She obviously hadn't seen Nigel trying to pitch his screenplay!

'It was nothing. Anyone would have done the same.'

As the beaming Miss Goldie gratefully embraced me,

the earth finally stopped moving. That's not supposed to happen. Absolutely typical!

Working with Miss Goldie was an absolute joy from beginning to end. She was incredibly supportive, helpful and selfless throughout. And in that particular scene I could say she was generous 'to a fault'. Ha! Ha!

During the making of the film, I decided I wanted somewhere of my own to live, although it meant leaving the luxurious surroundings of the Beverly Hills hotel. I rented a beachfront apartment in Venice Beach – a short distance from the studios. Described by the realtor as 'funky, zen-like and cool', it was indeed in a marvellous location. Situated on the boardwalk, with a balcony overlooking the beach, I could watch the scene unfold before me. Rollerbladers, joggers, musicians, hypnotists, breakdancers, comics and the occasional fire-eater created a unique carnival-like atmosphere.

I started rollerblading myself and before long had joined the surfing fraternity. I refrained from going completely blond but did purchase a wetsuit, a custom made, swallow tailed, pre-waxed 'Waikiki Superdude Board' and a bright red bandanna. I cut quite a dash, I can tell you. I was also pretty fit and Arnie – who by now had become a bit of a star and, I'm proud to say, a big friend – and I put on a few tricks for the crowds at Muscle Beach, the celebrated seafront gymnasium. I dined at Spago's and Chasen's and hung out with Jack Nicholson and the guys at the Lakers basketball games.

Fowl Play was a triumph and I was inundated with scripts and starring roles in more films: a western, *The Fox Bow Incident*; a remake of Dashiel Hammett's classic, *The Maltese Fox*; a romantic comedy, *When Basil Met Lori*; and a comedy gardening thriller featuring a privet detective – *Jagged Hedge*. I was delighted – and so was Uncle Louis – that they were all huge box office hits.

I was the toast of Hollywood and I was even honoured by having my paws imprinted into the forecourt of Mann's Chinese theatre, alongside all the Hollywood 'greats'.

Following the glittering success of my 'movies', television offers started to roll in and, remembering what Joan Collins had said about the small screen, I accepted lots of work. There was a guest part in *Miami Vice*, playing an urbane English villain involved in a model agency scam. I had to say things like, 'good Lord', and 'my dear chap'. That led to a part in *Magnum*. I was in an episode playing an urbane English villain – an artichoke farmer who was exploiting the Mexican farm labourers – and said things like, 'Great Scott!' and 'my dear fellow'. James Garner even came out of semi retirement especially for me and I guested in a *Rockford Files* special where I played an urbane English villain, a blackmailer, and said things like 'crumbs' and 'my dear old man'.

There was also the inevitable talk show circuit. All the chat shows were looking for a new David Niven figure, a sophisticated, worldly Englishman who had been around the block a few times and had the anecdotes to prove it. I dug out the tuxedo each time, even when I was on the breakfast shows, talked about my career and even gave a few amusing hints about my MI6 exploits. Obviously I couldn't be too specific in my denials, Official Secrets Act and all that, so the rumours took on a bit of a life of their own and I found the dinner invitations came even thicker and faster.

Although I was enjoying myself greatly, this hectic lifestyle was rather tiring and I decided I needed a holiday. Amazingly such an opportunity presented itself almost immediately and came from an unexpected source. Returning home from yet another fatiguing glitzy showbiz affair, there was a telegram waiting for me. It was from 'The Boss'. Sinatra not Springsteen.

BASIL, SAW YOU ON JOHNNY CARSON. YOU'RE A GAS. WE SHOULD GET TOGETHER. HOW ABOUT A LITTLE VACATION IN PALM SPRINGS? FRANK

It was an offer I couldn't refuse.

☆ ☆ ☆ ☆ ☆ ☆ ☆ ☆ ☆ ☆ ☆ ☆ ☆ ☆ ☆

CHAPTER TEN
VIVA LAS VEGAS

☆ ☆ ☆

'They sure would have made a beautiful couple. Basil and Maylene. They were just like Robin Hood and Maid Marian. I don't know what happened, where, or why it went wrong. One of those things, I guess. By the way, if any of the readers wish to tie that knot, we offer romance, beauty and sophistication and just a slice of history in our Sherwood Forest wedding chapel. Shoot an arrow of love in to the heart of your damsel and be for ever entwined by our own minister, Friar Tuck.'

'Little' John Schwartz, proprietor, Sherwood Forest Wedding Chapel and Casino

I was in a tight spot. Surrounded by water. In front of me an impassable forest. Behind me, rough terrain, and beyond that the merciless, unforgiving desert. I was trapped and had no idea how to get out.

'Your shot, Basil,' Frank Sinatra called over from the other side of the bunker. 'What's the matter, have you lost your ball?'

'No, it's all right – I've got my ball – it's the club I can't find.' With all my recent irons in the fire, I thought I had played my last golf game. Ha! Ha! However, I'd been persuaded to return to the links by Mister Frank, who wanted to set up a foursome with his friends Dean Martin and Ronald Reagan in Palm Springs.

'You go on, Mister Frank – I'll keep searching. I just can't see the wood for the trees. Boom! Boom!'

'Guys, I think it's my shot next.'

'Okay, Ronnie, go ahead.' Mister Frank held back.

Suddenly out of nowhere two dark-suited men, wearing sunglasses and carrying walkie-talkies appeared. I had wondered why they'd been hanging around and did think that they were dressed rather too formally to be caddies.

One of them offered a mobile telephone to the man about to putt. 'Mr President, it's for you. It's President Gorbachev.'

'Can you tell him to call back, Juan, this is an important shot.'

'I'm sorry, sir, but he said it was very important and mentioned something about an Arms Treaty.'

'Just tell him I'm busy. Oh . . . and if Ollie calls about the shredding – I don't remember anything about it. If Nancy wants me, I'm not here.'

So much for the great communicator.

Mister Ronnie addressed me as well as the ball, 'You know something, Basil, these people just don't realize how hard is to play this game without these interruptions. Putting is complicated enough without Gorby calling me about World War Three.'

I nodded agreeably at 'The Gipper' and offered him a jelly baby to aid his concentration. 'Thanks, Basil. Hey, these are pretty good. Remind me to send you some jelly beans.' Mr Ronnie looked at the hole and carefully measured the distance. He lifted the putter slowly and smoothly and sent the ball firmly into the middle of the hole.

'Good shot,' I said, thinking it might double the jelly bean consignment.

'Can we go to the nineteenth after this hole? I need a drink,' Mister Dean said plaintively.

'Dean, this is the *first* hole,' Mister Frank said, looking a bit fed up.

'Yeah, but I'm tired. I just got back from a six week run in Vegas.'

'Yeah, so what?'

'Well, soon, I'm going back for another six weeks. It's not that I'm such a good performer – I'm just a good loser.'

Mister Frank turned to me. 'They love him there. They gave him the keys to the city – but he's so stupid he locked himself out. Come on, Dean, just play your shot.'

'Okay.' A resigned Mister Dean was about to putt when he stopped and took off his hat, hand on heart. 'Fellas, let's just wait awhile.'

'Now what's the matter?' Even Mister Ronnie was getting impatient.

'Look over there.' Mister Dean pointed to a funeral cortege driving in the distance. Mister Frank was amazed. 'We've been playing this game for twenty years together and apart from stopping to have a quick slug from your hip flask, I've never ever seen you interrupt your game for anything.'

'Well,' Mister Dean replied, 'I think it's only right that I pay my respects. After all, I was married to her for ten years.'

Suddenly all hell let loose as a gunshot rang out. The secret servicemen flung themselves all over the place as more shots thudded into the nearby trees. The agent called Juan, who was hit in the arm, sent me sprawling into my golf trolley which in turn knocked into Mister Ronnie. He didn't seem to know what was happening and was still adding up his scorecard when my five iron fell out of the trolley and tripped him up, sending him tumbling to the ground. A bullet passed narrowly over his head. Then, the rest of the bodyguards sprang into action and sprinted in the direction of the would-be assassin while I tended to Juan. I saw that he was okay and had only suffered a flesh wound. He did, however, still need treatment. Coolly, I called out, 'We need some help over here. There's a hole in Juan.'

I did, in these circumstances, refrain from saying Boom! Boom!

Naturally, everyone was very pleased and grateful to me for saving the President's life with my quick thinking and over a celebratory dinner at Mister Frank's exquisite Palm Springs home that evening, Mister Frank put a proposition to me: 'Listen, Basil, why don't you stick around for a while. Maybe join *the pack*. You could even go over to Vegas – do a show whilst you're here.'

Now that was tempting. Although my film career was hugely successful, 'the roar of the greasepaint and the smell of the crowd' – or was it the other way around? I could never remember – somehow appealed to me even more at this time in my career. And it was also uncharted territory – yet another adventure that my dad would thoroughly approve of. 'That's very nice of you, Mister Frank. I'd be delighted. But how would it work out?'

'Don't worry. Leave everything to me. You and Vegas deserve each other. I'll fix it.'

And he did. Before I could say 'deuces are wild' I found myself working at a top Las Vegas venue. It was called 'The Englishman's Castle', a huge new casino and hotel complex built in the style of a British stately home, all roaring log fires, stuffed pheasants and wing-backed leather armchairs. The proportions of this stately home had been altered to accommodate a theatre that would seat 5,000 and a factory's worth of slot machines and gaming tables. There was a 'Mayfair Bar' and a 'Belgravia Coffee Shop'. The lobby was tricked out to look like Buckingham Palace and the valet parking area was an imitation of the Tower of London. There was more than a hint of Westminster Abbey about the gents toilets and the ladies was built in the style of Anne Hathaway's cottage. A distinct air of the Scottish Highlands blew around the swimming pool compound, including an impressive stag with antlers which received a daily wax and polish from the veterinary valeting service.

Liberace was topping the bill in the theatre because the management felt his kind of candelabra class was typical of the sort of evening entertainment the English upper classes would enjoy after their port and Stilton. I didn't like to tell them that most of the upper classes I'd met wouldn't have wanted him in their living rooms to dress the curtains, let alone tinkle on the ivories of any piano that might accidentally have found its way into the house.

I'd written a new routine for the booking, quoting a number of old favourites like Oscar Wilde, my dear friend Mister Noël and P.G. Wodehouse, in the hope of bringing a dash of genuine class to the proceedings, but felt Mister Liberace could help me with some tips on how to make my stage appearance just a bit more glamorous. Who better to teach me how to glitter than the most flamboyant figure in town?

'What you have to remember, Basil,' Mister Liberace said, taking a dainty sip from his piano-shaped porcelain teacup and dabbing his lips dry with a napkin, 'is that the people expect you to put on a show. They want you to be larger than life. If you sparkle brightly enough they'll forgive you anything. Nothing succeeds like excess. More tea?'

Quite surreally, a younger and almost identical version of Mister Liberace slid forward from the shadows and refilled my cup from a piano-shaped teapot. Mister Liberace wrinkled his nose up at the chap in a gesture of appreciation, a bit like a rabbit testing the early morning air for the scent of a predator. The young man drifted back into the shadows. I felt like I'd arrived at the very heart of the magic world of showbiz, that I was sitting in the presence of the very spirit of entertainment himself.

'Don't you think Scott's gorgeous?' Mister Liberace asked me. 'Did you know that I'm having plastic surgery so that I can look just like him? If you don't mind me saying, you could use some yourself.'

'Actually the only plastic surgery I'm likely to undergo is if I cut up my credit card. Ha! Ha!'

'Oh, that's so funny. But I'm serious. A little nip or tuck would do wonders for you.'

I felt like giving him a nip of another kind, but I decided instead to change the subject. 'Do you think I should consider a new stage costume, Mister Liberace?' I enquired, munching on a feather-light macaroon, aware that the crumbs were floating down towards the immaculate white carpet on his dressing room floor.

'Please call me Lee,' he smiled, his teeth sparkling from the lights that surrounded the mirrors above the dressing table.

What a smile. I felt that I knew each of his teeth personally. 'And you must call me Basil,' I replied.

'Well, Mister Basil,' he leaned forward, about to impart some priceless secrets from the vaults of his experience in pleasing crowds. 'It is my belief that in Las Vegas you can never have too many sequins. I slip into something spectacular at least half a dozen times during the show. Something like this.' He pointed to a long clothes rack and, more specifically, to a pink suit embroidered with silver translucent beads. 'They illuminate during the encore.'

'I see.' I'd realized the moment I hit town that I was now a long way away from Frinton. The sequins idea wasn't bad and I made a mental note to speak to my wardrobe people. Mister Lee also very sweetly lent me some of his jewellery, although he wisely insisted that I sign a receipt for it before leaving the room.

As I got to know him better, during the engagement, we decided to perform a duet on the show. We worked on a couple of musical numbers in which he could accompany me on the piano. We had decided to do 'My Way', and 'Don't Put Your Daughter on the Stage Mrs Worthington'. We were also working on a routine which would hark back to the days of my double acts with Mister Rodney, Mister Derek and the others, with Lee tinkling on the keys as we talked and me sitting on top of his pink sequinned grand. It seemed to be working out quite well – lots of jokes about him liking fox fur and me trying on his rings.

By now, I had moved into a suite at the hotel and as I hadn't seen Mister Frank for a while, I invited him to the show. A lot of people in town had less than generous things to say about the Governor, as he described himself, although they never seemed to say them when he was around. He'd always been very kind to me and, of course, I'd reciprocated his invitation by suggesting he come and visit me in England some time. He surprised me by saying he had always wanted to see Norfolk. Then I realized what he meant. He'd heard that there were some 'terrific broads' there. Ha! Ha!

When I sang 'My Way' with Lee at the end of our set I consciously tried to model my phrasing on Mister Frank's (if you're going to learn, you should always learn from the best), and I was extremely chuffed when the man himself made a surprise spontaneous guest appearance and sang along with us.

I decided I should have a line of chorus girls backing me on stage, and that they should all be garbed in gold foxes' heads and tails, with smart little waistcoats and capes in a pastiche of my own style. They were all delightful looking women and I must say it was like permanently living on the set of a musical like *Sweet Charity* or *Gypsy*.

I have to confess that I fell for one of the girls myself. She was a cute little vixen called Maylene. She was from Missouri and said that she was the first one in the family to escape the trailer park and make it in show business. I found this idea of the family and their gypsy like existence very romantic, and she herself looked a little like Cher in her earlier days.

We'd been knocking about together for a few months – much to the chagrin of some of the other girls – when I realized that Maylene just wasn't the one for me. We came from such varying backgrounds, cultures – even countries. It was like we were from two different worlds. When the initial feelings of romance had gone, there was very little left between us. The relationship had lost its passion and although I tried a little ardour – little ardour Ha! Ha! – I knew deep down it just wasn't to be.

Maylene had, rather worryingly, even been talking about tying the knot but it was hopeless. By then, we just didn't have enough in common to be together for a few hours, never mind the rest of our lives. I knew, before I broke her heart, I would have to tell her the awful truth. She was a sweet young thing and I didn't want to hurt her.

One night, when I was going to break the bad news, she told me that we'd been invited to a fancy dress party being held at midnight on 'the strip'. Not exactly being in the mood, I said I wasn't very keen on the idea, but she begged me to go. I reluctantly agreed. Apparently we were to go dressed as Robin Hood and Maid Marian and Maylene had already arranged the costumes. I had always fancied myself as a bit of an Errol Flynn and, once adorned in Lincoln green, my mood brightened. I suppose I should have become suspicious when, on the way there, she confided that the party was being held in one of those dreadful casino wedding chapels. I thought nothing of it until we arrived to be met at the door by a large, rotund character in the guise of Friar Tuck, beaming happily. In fact, everyone seemed to be straight out of Sherwood Forest – it was obviously a themed fancy dress party. I did wonder why all of Maylene's girlfriends from the chorus were there dressed as outlaws and why her father, Jed, was present and done up as the Sheriff of Nottingham.

Friar Tuck appeared again, this time clutching a huge ham hock in one hand and a Bible in the other and led me centre stage down the aisle where a veiled Maylene waited. The monk then started asking me lots of questions about current commitments and relationships and talking about 'contractual impediments'. There was also a keyboard player hanging about – it wasn't Mister Lee but a strange chap in the shape of an Allan-a-Dale lookalike.

I finally realized what was going on . . . I had been completely duped. Maylene was trying to get me to open in another show and perform at a rival venue – for free. This could seriously jeopardize my exclusive agreement with my current employers. I couldn't believe that she would stoop so low and I left the casino chapel immediately. It was indeed a lucky escape and, but for my quick thinking, I could have been seriously compromised.

And maybe even married! Ha! Ha!

Apart from this unfortunate incident, life in Las Vegas was by no means unpleasant. To start with there was constant room service, and then there were the other ex-pats in town. Tom Jones and Engelbert Humperdinck were often hanging around the suite, along with feisty Shirley Bassey. The only problem seemed to be with some of my material. Being an old pro, I could tell the Vegas audiences, poor old dears, didn't really get all my jokes. They laughed politely, but I knew that my act was a bit too sophisticated for them. Despite the obvious slant of the Englishman's castle, I decided to do the sort of gags that they would understand. I'd changed part of my image to suit the glitzy desert town, it was now time to change the patter. I spent one whole night re-writing everything and the following evening did my new act. Mister Lee was spellbound as I launched into my new material:

'Good evening, ladies and gentlemen. Did you know that I originally came to Vegas for a change and a rest – the one armed bandits got the change and the croupiers got the rest. A friend of mine brought his wife to Vegas – he'd heard that you lose everything here. It's the place where wallets go to die. And it's true, they really see you coming and take advantage – even the trees rub their palms together. I parked my car on a meter – I put a coin in, it came up three lemons, and I lost the car.' And so on. The crowds loved it and I was an even bigger hit. I was offered a longer contract which I gratefully accepted.

Uncle Louis still wanted me back in Hollywood and said that he'd had some very interesting offers. He was in constant contact and desperate for me to return and bolster the studio output. But I'd realized that the silver screen didn't satisfy my need for a live performance. I loved playing the audience and getting the buzz of an immediate reaction whatever I did. As a favour to Uncle Louis, however, I had actually returned to Twenty-First Century Fox briefly to star in one of their major features. The film, *Raging Fox,* was the story of a once great boxer, having gone to seed somewhat and having put on lots of poundage – even though he was still a heavyweight contender. The role of the podgy pugilist was quite challenging, especially as I'd decided to forego a body double and, through a selfless diet of jelly babies and toffees, actually put on the flab myself.

Of course the film was a huge success and for a while I basked in the glow of critical acclaim. But then, back in Vegas, sitting around the suite all day with the guys, eating and drinking, I noticed the weight just wasn't coming off. To try to distract the audience's attention from my tubbier parts I kept having more and more sequins sewn on to the outfits.

As usual fate was on my side; Uncle Louis had given up on my permanent return to Hollywood and so had given my name to a Broadway producer by the name of Joel Daniels. He came to see me at the hotel one night after the show. It was rather embarrassing actually – he walked in to my dressing room and caught me looking at myself sideways in the mirror, smoothing one paw over my admittedly rounded tummy.

'You'll need to shape up – just a tad,' Joel said, eyeing me critically.

'What for?'

'You can't hit Broadway looking quite like that.'

I was puzzled, 'Broadway?'

'Didn't Louis explain?'

'No, he did not.'

'We're doing a musical version of *The Elephant Man* on Broadway and we really want you to star. We loved your movies and we think we have the right vehicle for you. This show is going to be huge and we want you to be a part of it. But you have to be in tip top condition – as you English say.'

I was annoyed to say the least, 'Are you insinuating that I'm fat, Mr Daniels?'

Mr Daniels looked shocked, 'Did I say you were fat? I didn't say you were fat. You're not fat. Fat is when you have a shower and your feet don't get wet. That's fat. You just need to tone up a little – lose a few pounds here and there – mostly there.' He pointed to my tummy which I had been unable to hold in any longer and continued before I had time to open my mouth. 'You, Basil, are a shining star in Hollywood and we are going to make you an even brighter star on Broadway. Take care. I'll be in touch.'

With that, he turned on his heel and left. I was pretty taken aback by the impertinence. We hadn't even talked money. But a Broadway musical! That was worth thinking about. And he wasn't completely off the mark about my physical condition. There was nothing for it but to launch a strict 'get fit' campaign.

So the regime began. I joined a gym, started jogging in the midday desert sun and pumped iron until I had muscles in places I didn't even know I had places. The pounds fell off and yet again I was the lean, mean machine that I had been whilst living in Los Angeles. I was back in peak condition and felt that I could perform at the top of my form once more.

The prospect of a new professional challenge was exciting. In fact, it was just what I needed. Broadway beckoned and like Mister Frank himself says, 'If you can make it there, you can make it anywhere.' I knew that if I was to move to New York to appear in *The Elephant Man*, there was one very important thing that I had to do; I had to pack my trunk. Ha! Ha!

☆ ☆ ☆ ☆ ☆ ☆ ☆ ☆ ☆ ☆ ☆ ☆ ☆ ☆

CHAPTER ELEVEN
THE BIG APPLE

☆ ☆ ☆

'Broadway has surely found its next long running musical in *The Elephant Man* and in Englishman Basil Brush, New York has discovered a shimmering, stunning, sensational star. Basil bursts with brio and bathos in his portrayal as unfortunate misfit John Merrick. I can't wait to see more of him – especially out of that make-up! Move over Gene Kelly, Fred Astaire, Donald O'Connor – there's a new song and dance man in town and he's called . . . Basil Brush.

Rick La Fontaine, Theatre Critic,
Manhattan Gazette

I was in the most marvellous shape and feeling better than I had been for some time. My confidence was further boosted by the VIP treatment I was given on the plane to New York. I had my own compartment, cinema screen, stewardess and as much cream soda (slimline) and as many jelly babies (sugar free) as I required. But I was actually much too excited to indulge myself and so looking forward to my next adventure.

If you are a Londoner, Broadway means Hammersmith or Cricklewood. If, like me, you hail from the countryside, Broadway is a picturesque spot in the Cotswolds much frequented by American tourists. There are also two beautiful villages known as the 'The Slaughters' – Upper and Lower – and again, Americans have so fallen in love with the hamlets that they have tried to buy them and transport them across the Atlantic. Presumably to have the Slaughters on Tenth Avenue. Ha! Ha!

But I digress. Because I am on my way to Broadway, New York. The Great White Way. The home of 'Theatreland'. And where, incidentally, I'm going to have my name up in lights. If the show is successful, then I shall be here for some time. But if the 'Butchers of Broadway', as the famously vitriolic New York critics are known, carve the show up into little pieces, then I will be on my way – to who knows where?

When the script arrived for *The Elephant Man*, it appropriately weighed a ton and it brought to mind an occasion when a friend of mine was offered a musical of the telephone directory. As I said to him at the time, 'Not much of a plot, but there's a lot of good numbers in it – and a huge cast.' Ha! Ha!

My spirits took a slight dip when I stepped off the plane at Kennedy airport and who should be there to meet me but my old chauffeur from Twenty-First Century Fox. Yes, it was none other than Quinn, who had been hired by the show's producer to whisk me to a discreet little hotel on the Upper East Side.

He was clearly pleased to see me. 'Hi Baz, how are they hanging?'

'Mustn't grumble,' I answered somewhat non-committedly and quickly changed the subject. 'Now, the last time I saw you, Quinn, you were about to drive here from Los Angeles. How did it go?'

'The drive was great, Basil. I did that in four days. But the whole trip lasted two weeks because it took me ten days to fold the maps.'

Not a bad gag, I thought, and one I hadn't heard before. 'What happened to the pink limo?'

'Oh, I swapped it for this Japanese compact. You need a small car here. Easier to find a parking place. Otherwise it's just impossible.'

'Ah . . . parking is such sweet sorrow. Ha! Ha!'

'Good one, Basil. Actually that's not the only problem I have with my wheels. I just washed the car and I can't do a thing with it. Did you know, Basil, that they just passed a new law here? Any car going over thirty miles per hour must have a driver.'

'Ha! Ha! Quinn, you're in good form.'

'It's New York, man – it's a great town. I'm doing some stand-up in the village, come and see me sometime.'

The city had given Quinn an edge. He seemed almost a different chap from before. If the 'Big Apple' was going to have the same effect on me, I could see New York was going to be my kind of town. Having said my farewells and made a promise to catch his act, I 'hung my hat' – a rather fetching panama – in the Benchley Hotel, the place that was going to be yet another temporary home. Recently, I had been in more hotel rooms than a Gideon's Bible. Ha! Ha!

As soon as the media heard I was in town there was a queue of journalists knocking on the door. I had Joel Daniels, the show's producer, control the situation by insisting on copy approval and cover photos. I was surprised how many of them were willing to comply. And, of course, once you've been on the cover of *Vanity Fair* it isn't long before the society folk start ringing with the invitations. Jackie O was the first to call. She was established in publishing by then, having given up marrying, and was keen to talk about possible projects. She seemed a sweet woman, although she went very quiet when I mentioned my old friend, Mister Frank. I think there may have been some bad blood there with her first husband and father-in-law, but I never quite got to the bottom of the whole thing. We talked a lot about fitness and diet and she made me promise to come jogging with her in Central Park the next morning. It was, in fact, Miss Jackie who first suggested that I produce an exercise video, *Working It Out With Basil* – an aerobic extravaganza with guest appearances from lots of my showbiz pals. Even Mister Frank took a turn in a leotard but I could never make him stick to the routine. He said he preferred to do it his way. It soon became a top seller in the video market thanks to Mr Joel's contacts in the business. Soon, we had a whole array of leotards, T-shirts and headbands under the title of 'Brushwear' endorsed with my name and logo. I must say it was a nice little earner, augmenting my Broadway salary, and the required personal appearances kept me in pretty good nick.

Rehearsals of *The Elephant Man*, which started within a week of my arrival, took place in a room over The Footlights Deli in downtown Manhattan. I entered with some trepidation but was put at ease by the friendliness and warmth of the assembled cast who immediately burst into spontaneous applause. Soon, the pianist was bashing out some of the music on an upright – believe me, he was

no Liberace – and we went through the musical numbers.
I began to feel the old adrenaline coursing through my
veins once more. The songs were terrific. Lots of show-
stoppers. The opening chorus by the entire cast was an
ensemble number called 'Mumbo Jumbo', and there was
a memorable and rather sad ballad entitled 'They say that
an elephant never forgets, but then there's not much to
remember' and an exciting dance routine, 'Stampede'.
But the hit of the show, and the song that was expected to
bring the house down, was my poignant solo number, 'I'm
a Human Being Not an Animal'. At the time, Mister Joel
said, 'You'll take about six curtains – and listen, save two
for me, I'm refurnishing my apartment.'

Here's an extract:

> *Verse:* I hate all that staring
> The whisper and glaring
> The taunting and teasing's begun
> Their lives must be sad
> But it gets really bad
> When they come up and give me a bun.

> *Chorus:* Oh God, the enormity
> Of his deformity
> Is making life so hard to bear
> Doctors say and we quote
> There is no antidote
> And surgeons hang their heads in despair.

Day after day, week after week, we worked on the
show. It was all coming together. Surprisingly, John Hurt
turned up one day at rehearsals to see how we were getting

on. I'd always thought he had made a very good job of playing my part, John Merrick, in the film and wondered why he hadn't got the stage part. So, apparently, did he.

'It's like Audrey Hepburn and Julie Andrews in reverse,' he remarked to me in a quiet moment, referring to the assumption that Julie Andrews would get the lead in the film of *My Fair Lady* because of her performance in the stage version. I felt quite sorry for him but he said in one way he was relieved and muttered something about 'the nightmare of all that make-up', and warned me about 'life in the sack not being all that wonderful'.

I told him I was really looking forward to the scene in which John Merrick dies. I knew I was going to be great. After all, I'd had enough practice of 'dying on stage'. Boom! Boom!

Finally, it was opening night. Imagine that – my Broadway debut! Backstage that evening, the atmosphere was electric. Everyone was tense – the only light relief was provided by one of the dancers, Gordon, who held up one of his hands: 'I'm not saying I'm nervous, but see this little finger, well, it used to be my thumb.'

The overture was at an end, a few coughs out front. Then a short but ominous silence. There's a breathless hush in the stalls tonight. The houselights go down. Curtain up. Applause.

As I made my entrance after the opening dance routine, the terror which had been building up for all those weeks disappeared – the nervous anxiety remained and then the adrenaline took over. When I removed the sack to reveal my horrible features (yes, I was wearing the hideous make-up in case you're asking) there was a gasp from the audience and I knew I had them under my spell as they surrendered themselves to the magic of the theatre.

The crowd were right with me as I sang my first number and I received appreciative applause. As the show moved on from scene to scene, I was firmly focussed on my performance but surprisingly still aware of the odd distraction: the rustling of sweet papers, the coughers who should have stayed home and the chatterers who offered a running commentary for those who may have missed any dialogue, not for a moment imagining that the dialogue was missed because they were talking.

And, of course, all the time I was completely dependent on my cues and the professionalism of the other actors. Luckily we were all word perfect and everyone was marvellous. As the show progressed we felt more and more warmth from the audience. The butterflies in our tummies had flown away to be replaced by bees buzzing with excitement. We sensed success. At the final curtain, even the standing ovations were getting standing ovations.

The ecstatic applause and cheering was deafening – so loud, in fact, that the actors in the next theatre took six extra bows.

I got to the opening night party with the applause and cheering still ringing in my ears. It was held at the famous showbiz haunt, Sardi's restaurant, where we spent the night nervously awaiting the early morning reviews. Finally the runner arrived with a bundle of papers under his arm. There was much grabbing, rustling of turning pages and snippets read out: 'Elephant man – Big Hit', 'Box Office Boom! Boom!', 'Brush sweeps audience off their feet', 'First night hysterics for Merrick'. The verdict was unanimous. We were a hit. And on a more personal note, this anonymous review in the *New York Times*: 'Basil

Brush, the celebrated wit, raconteur, stand-up comic and film star, last night took on a dramatic role that was both challenging and demanding. He jumped in with both sets of feet and came out victorious. He played the part with panache and pathos, vividly portraying the pathetic figure of John Merrick. There wasn't a dry eye in the house when Merrick died and even here Brush managed to breathe life into the death scene.'

Not bad, eh? And I promise I didn't write it myself!

Within a very short time of my arrival in the city, I found myself completely at home in New York. I loved the pace, buzz and ambience of the city. Everyone was a wise-cracking wiseguy and I was in my element. I was taking a huge bite out of 'The Big Apple' and enjoying its sweet juicy taste. There was culture on the streets everywhere – although the mayor had promised to do something about that. Ha! Ha! I found myself hanging out at the Met and the Guggenheim and I also went to the Bronx zoo. I tried out some jokes on the animals – what an audience – I had them eating out of my hand. Boom! Boom! I even tried the ballet, although, I have to admit I just didn't enjoy it. In fact, the whole thing made me nervous – I couldn't tell which side was winning. Ha! Ha! I also couldn't under-stand why all those dancers ran around on tiptoes. Why don't they get just get taller people to start with?

Then, out of the blue, Woody Allen rang and asked if I would like to come down to Michael's Pub, the club where he played clarinet in a jazz band every Monday night. I had always been an admirer of his and he assured me the feeling was mutual! I was delighted by his invitation.

THE BIG APPLE

After wrangling a night off from the theatre, I found myself at a table in front of the stage and, although I've always been more of a be bopper than a traditionalist, I thoroughly enjoyed myself. Mister Woody certainly knocked Acker Bilk into a cocked hat – or bowler hat, I should say. I also got the shock of my life when he asked me to 'sit in' on drums. I hadn't played for years but, fortunately, he played a slow number which suited me very well. I suppose he must have heard I was well known for my 'Brush work.' Ha! Ha!

After the show, he joined me for a chat. 'It's a great pleasure to meet you, Basil. No really it is. I've been a fan of yours for many years.'

'Mister Woody, the feeling is mutual.'

'You're a show business legend. It's not like you just show up and perform. An act like that takes years to perfect. Believe me, I know these things. And I can tell you're a good person.'

'Well, I try to uphold a certain old-world dignity and behaviour that sometimes seems . . .'

Mister Woody continued relentlessly, 'I bet you sleep well. Have you ever noticed that good people sleep well but bad people seem to have more fun when they're awake?'

'Oh, I have a lot of fun, Mister Woody, I can assure you of that.'

'I never have. Everything has always conspired against me. Even when I was at school, I failed to make the marbles team because of my height.'

'But surely you must have some enjoyable times now?'

'It's not true, Basil. One of my ex-girlfriends has just sold the secrets of our sex life to a publisher. They're going to make a board game out of it. She's so vain that on her own birthday, she sends her mother a congratulations card. But enough about me. I hear you're in a Broadway musical – that's great, I've always wanted to do that. In fact I once auditioned for *Guys and Dolls*. I wanted to be one of the dolls.'

I wasn't used to being the straight man, but I suppose he was one of the world's funniest entertainers and I could tell he genuinely liked me. Unfortunately before I could get a word in edgewise, Mister Woody was called back to the bandstand. 'Hey, let's stay in touch. Get your therapist to call my therapist.'

Funnily enough whilst I was living in LA I had toyed with the idea of getting a therapist. It wasn't that I had some psychological problem that needed sorting – it was more of a status thing. It seemed everyone in the business had a therapist, analyst or shrink. Mister Woody was a great advocate of this world although he did admit that even after twenty-five years of therapy, 'It was still going slowly.' He recommended me to a therapist – not his own, of course – and I started going twice a week for the statutory fifty-minute sessions. My therapist, Miss Marilyn Edelstein, tried desperately to find some phobia, unusual behavioural trait or deep-seated anxiety.

'I'm sorry, I can't help you there. My life just isn't a bed of neuroses,' I told her.

'But you must have something that you don't like about yourself and want to share with me.'

'Well, I bite my nails a bit much when I'm a bit nervous.'

'Ah ha.'

'Yes, so much so, I think my stomach needs a manicure. Ha! Ha!'

I thought Miss Edelstein might be annoyed at my flippant attitude but surprisingly she just laughed and wrote something down in her notebook. The only thing I did admit to was the occasional pang of sibling rivalry when I was a child.

'Well, with about thirty brothers and sisters, it's not surprising, is it?' She seemed tickled by this and was lost in thought for a while. I have to say, I thoroughly enjoyed this time to reflect on my life and pour out my innermost feelings. She just listened intently to my garrulous confessions and took copious notes – a knowing smile on her lips. It was not long before she started to record the sessions.

But after a while, things started to go wrong and the relationship seemed to sour. I once arrived ten minutes late for a session and discovered that she'd started without me. As I entered the consulting room, I heard her repeating out loud what I'd said the week before.

Eventually, we had to finish the therapy sessions altogether. It was entirely her decision. Miss Edelstein admitted that she was in love with me. A fact of which I was completely unaware. She described it as a 'classic case of counter transference'. There was nothing that could be done. Never could I see her again. It was all very upsetting but not nearly as distressing as when I bumped into her at the cabaret lounge of the Carlyle Hotel and found that she had given up the therapy business and was doing my act – badly!

It was during this time that, surprisingly, Mister Woody, who usually writes all his own scripts announced to me that he was suffering from writer's block and asked me to contribute some material for his latest film *Everything You Wanted to Know About Going Bananas in Manhattan*. Of course I was flattered and delighted to be asked and he seemed very pleased with the gags and scenarios I wrote for him. As a result, over the years, he asked me to play several cameo roles in some more of his movies.

Of course, once word got out that I'd appeared in a few of Woody's films I was approached by a number of production companies to return to the silver screen in a starring role. Some of them were pretty small scale and although I had no objection to some of the more arty, aspiring independents trying their luck, I could soon tell which ones to avoid.

There was, for example, a video concern called Armchair Adventures with a rather catchy slogan 'epics without ethics'. They specialized in low budget remakes of the classics. Some of their titles included *Eleven Dalmatians*, *Gone With The Breeze*, *Guess Who's Coming To Nibbles*, *Raiders of The Lost Canoe* and *The Thirty-two Steps*.

It gave me the idea for a similar selection of musicals that might prove to have a cult following. There was the Mormon musical, *Forty-Nine Brides for Seven Brothers*; the Russian musical, *Singing In The Ukraine*; an all-singing all-dancing production of Salvador's surreal life, *Hello Dali*; the Russian Revolutionary epic set to music, *Czar Wars*; the musical mammoth shopping expedition, *Store Trek* and the breakfast musical, *The Sound Of Muesli*. Needless to say, they have yet to be made. Ha! Ha!

As the months slipped into years, *Elephant Man* continued to be a huge success. What had started as a six-month engagement had now become an almost permanent contract – and we were still packing in the punters and taking bookings for years ahead. It seemed that New York had become my permanent home. I had a whole new entourage and circle of friends and, although I missed my family, I made sure that I telephoned my parents every Sunday. They were both so delighted for me and my dad was especially proud of all my achievements.

I loved living in New York – it had an atmosphere and pace that was unique and there was always something to do. 'The city that never sleeps' is a very apt description and the nightlife is simply incomparable. Often after the show, with the adrenaline still flowing, I would seek out some club and dance the night away to the latest sounds. One night whilst hanging out at my favourite Manhattan haunt, The House Of House, this rather stunning young woman wended her way over to where I was quietly watching the proceedings. To my amazement, it turned out to be none other than the material girl herself, Madonna.

'Hi, beautiful stranger. Come on, let's dance.' She grabbed my paw and led me to the centre of the floor where she proceeded to dance in a most unusual manner. This was marvellous. I'd always been a great fan of hers since the days when she used to wear traffic cones across her chest – and I could see why now: she certainly was something of a diversion. Ha! Ha!

'Do you like garage?' The Queen of Pop grabbed both my hands and pulled me daintily towards her.

'I'm quite fond of the odd NCP but not enough to lose sleep over,' I replied. Madonna danced on in a way that could only be described as mesmeric.

'How about techno?'

'Oh yes, now *that* I do quite enjoy, although I find it lacks emotion. Now, if you could give a techno feel to some of your own songs, well, I think that might be a rather an innovative combination. And probably more interesting than the imagery in *Erotica* which, to be perfectly honest, I found rather annoying.' I thought I might have over-stepped the mark, but Madonna immediately stopped in her tracks, bringing the whole of the dance floor to a halt.

'That's brilliant.'

'Ah . . . how nice of you to say so. Well, if I've brought a ray of light into your creative darkness—'

'And that is going to be my title. You – whoever you are – are a genius.'

'Basil Brush. Pleased to meet you.'

After that first meeting, Madonna and I became fast friends. We would hang out together, go shopping and I would advise her on her latest togs. She admired my tweeds and I thought that she would suit something in tartan. Madonna said she would bear it in mind for the future.

We often used to find ourselves meeting of an afternoon at the famous Russian Tea Rooms, Madonna holding forth on her latest spiritual dilemma – whether to pursue the mediaeval Jewish religion of Kabbalah or whether to go with Zoroastrianism which had taken its hold on some of the residents of the Upper West Side. For my part, I would bemoan the fact that the waiters in the Russian Tea Rooms were loath to put milk in the tea and when they did, it was always served in a glass. Extraordinary.

Still, it was a lot of fun and sometimes her new beau, a Brit called Guy Ritchie, would join us. He had written, and was about to direct, his first feature film. I gave him a few hints and he seemed genuinely grateful. In fact, he wanted me to star in it and was going to call it *Lock, Fox and Two Smoking Basils*. However, when I read the script I decided it wasn't my type of film – too much violence – and so I turned the part down. I think he was disappointed and I'm not sure that the film ever got made. We did all, however, become very close pals and once at a dinner party when Madonna slipped out to powder her nose I told Mister Guy that she was a very nice girl and that he ought to make an honest woman of her. He looked at me rather strangely, but I think he knew what I meant.

I was disappointed that I never did get to record with the future Mrs Ritchie, but working in the musical had given my confidence as a singer a huge boost and I went on to record duets with some of the top female vocalists such as Shania Twain, The Dixie Chicks and Britney Spears. I was even approached to write and record 'a rap' with Dr Snoop Doggy Dog Magic Puff Puff:

Now my father was a brush and my mother was a
    broom
And when I tell a corny gag I go 'Boom! Boom!'
I was raised in the country ever since I was a cub
Knew every blade of grass and every village pub
The Brushes were descended from good yeomen
    stock
I was quite a snappy dresser – never used to wear
    a smock
The girls all pursued me, said reliable sources
But then when they chased me
They were all riding horses
I'm bright eyed and bushy tailed – A cheeky sort
    of chap
And I want you all to listen to my Boom! Boom! rap

Now I had this ambition to reach the dizzy heights
And I knew maybe someday I would see my name
    in lights

From camp entertainer to television star
And wherever one goes people know who you are
Well, soon I had the sort of news to please all the fans
The magic name of Hollywood featured in my plans
A movie with the cutest little kid ever born
And if you don't believe it's me – just ask Goldie Hawn
From there to Las Vegas and Sinatra's tender trap
Where the Godfather joins me in the Boom! Boom!
    rap

A duet in Las Vegas – now that's something I can
    handle
Then I found out I was playing second fiddle to a
    candle
Liberace at the piano in a cloud of fluffy feather
I responded with a sou'wester representing British
    weather
All the same we hit it off and we soon became good
    friends
And sad to say, it wasn't long before his chapter ends
Time to move on to New York where a musical awaits
An p'raps it's time for me to take my place amongst
    the greats
Another town, another gig, a milestone on the map
That's the odyssey of Basil with his Boom! Boom! rap

Now I'm quite a city slicker in New York, New York
'Cos I'm flipping my lid and I'm popping my cork
And if you don't think Baz has razzmatazz
See me razzle-dazzle 'em with all that jazz
Took the place by storm – and what do you know
Got the starring role in a Broadway show

Who knows I could end up as a lord or earl
The world is my oyster with a huge big pearl
In my t-shirt, trainers and my baseball cap
I'm signing off now with my Boom! Boom! rap!

Being involved in this project was quite an experience, I can tell you. Amazingly, we went 'platinum' (could someone please explain what that means?) and the single was a huge hit in the clubs.

Although *The Elephant Man* was still going very well and heading into its second decade, I realized that I was becoming stale. If I played the part of John Merrick much longer, I would be typecast for ever. The success of the rap had shown that there were other paths to follow. I was also emotionally and physically tired and was reminded of Mr Hurt's warnings – there is a limit to the number of hours a person can spend under hot lights with their head in an old flour sack. The applause was wonderful but I would gladly have swapped it for a couple of full lungs of oxygen at times.

Whilst I was deliberating my next move, fate dealt another dramatic twist. I had a call from my mother – Dad was dangerously ill. I must return to England at once. I suddenly realized how much I missed my family and came to an immediate and life-changing decision. I was going to go home for good. I told Mister Joel that I wanted to be released from my contract. He was naturally disappointed, but seemed to understand how I felt. Being an experienced producer he had realized that I couldn't go on for ever and had already taken the sensible precaution of lining someone else up. Apparently a rising star – another English fox called Fred.

Surely, it couldn't be? No . . . it's not possible. Anyway

there was no time to find out. I had to leave New York quickly. There was only just enough time to give my final regards to Broadway.

EPILOGUE

THE BRUSH IS BACK

'There is in the Englishman a combination of qualities, a modesty, an independence, a responsibility, a repose, combined with an absence of everything calculated to call a blush in to the cheek of a young person, which one would seek in vain among the Nations of Earth.'

Charles Dickens, *Our Mutual Friend*

'Basil is so English that if he ever cut himself, he would have bled tea.'

Anonymous American

By the time I arrived back home in England and reached the family den, it was too late. My father had died. I was devastated. I'd always thought that dad would last for ever. Now, I'd never see him again.

My mother was naturally sorrowful but also stoical and showed her true show business colours. The credo that 'the show must go on' had never been tested so rigorously. The funeral was to be a few days later in the orchard where in his prime Dad had liked to chase rabbits and in his later years had watched many a sunset with my mother beside him.

'Would you say a few words, Basil?' Mum had asked. 'Your dad would have liked that. He was so proud of you and your career.'

'Of course,' I replied.

I wasn't surprised by the number of people who turned up for the service – everyone loved Dad. When the time came to pay my respects, I was a little afraid that my voice wouldn't make it, for all the professional training. I climbed into the branches of one of the apple trees and surveyed the sea of upturned faces; twenty or thirty generations of Brushes and other related clans, all hanging on my words.

'When I was a cub,' I said, 'it was my dad who first nurtured my interest in comedy and encouraged me to pursue a career in show business. He always supported me in whatever I did and I'll always be grateful to him for that. But above all, he told all his children that life was a wonderful adventure, to be enjoyed to the full. He was a great teacher and he taught me well.

'Dad wasn't afraid of dying but in the words of one of my greatest friends, Woody Allen, "he just didn't want to be there when it happened".' There was, of course, a lot more that I wanted to say, but I couldn't get any more words out – I was just too emotional.

After Dad 'had gone to earth' we all returned to the

den. That evening, we partied in his honour – just as he would have wanted. It was a pretty noisy, rumbustious gathering with lots of joke telling, communal singing and heartfelt toasts to the memory of Ivan Brush.

For the next few weeks I stayed in the den, supporting my mother and younger siblings who were still in a state of shock. At this time of reflection, I decided to sort out some of my old personal belongings. In a suitcase full of correspondence I found fan letters that had been written to me over the years. Eulogies from admirers of all ages, including those from past prime ministers, foreign secretaries, theatrical knights and even members of Abba!

There was one envelope, somewhat yellowing and dusty, that had never been opened. My mother must have filed it away years ago. It was postmarked 'Buckingham Palace'. I tore it open and read the contents;

Dear Mr Brush,
Please excuse this hand-written missive but my equerry has gone missing – probably been at the cooking sherry again.
Her Royal Majesty, Queen Elizabeth the Second (That's me! Hello!) is mindful of your service to the nation and wishes it be known that if you are equally minded to . . . oh, dash it . . . look the thing is . . . we wondered if we could possibly confer upon you one of our special gongs – officially it's called something like 'The Most Excellent Order Of The British Empire'. In other words – a knighthood.
You know, in return for that little business you took care of in Jamaica.

Anyway, let me know if you accept. By 'Return' would be convenient. Use my post – you know, 'The Royal Mail'.

Kind Regards
Elizabeth R

PS Mummy says hello and how about a game of brag sometime!

Well, the Queen Mother had come through. Only, it seemed I was about twenty years too late to accept her daughter's kind offer! But that wasn't entirely the point. I had been offered the knighthood and that's what really mattered.

Although these were particularly sad circumstances, it felt marvellous to be back home for good. Whilst domiciled in America, I'd been home for a few visits of course. I once popped back at the request of my old chum Prince Charles who wanted me to perform at his eldest son's birthday party at Kensington Palace.

I had also come home to receive a BAFTA lifetime achievement award, which was absolutely lovely. It was extremely generous of them and I don't mind telling you that I broke down and cried at the ceremony. This was mainly because the members of the Academy, in their wisdom, had invited Harry Burns to present the award. Apparently, he'd been extradited from Brazil, had served his time and was now fully rehabilitated as Head of Comedy at ITV.

On another trip home, I had struck up a close friendship with 'Posh Vulpes' – a delightful, pouting member of an all girl singing group. I met her playing leapfrog and I just couldn't get over her. Ha! Ha! But it just didn't work out. It was the time of rampant 'Vixen power' and the publicity was too much even for me to endure. So, we parted.

Apart from one trip north of the border to attend Mister Guy and Madonna's wedding, I was now enjoying myself just being at home with the family and meeting some of my new cousins and nephews. If you think rabbits multiply untidily, you should see how bad foxes are about leaving litters all over the place. Ha! Ha! I had plenty of savings and after my exertions on Broadway, needed a long break.

And then the call came, out of the blue as it always does. An independent production company wanted me to star in a sitcom. They thought that the time was right for me to make a comeback and I was happy to accept their offer. Apparently I was a cross between a 'National Treasure' and a 'British Institution' – I described it as a sort of 'A Jewel in a Bowl of Brown Windsor Soup'. Ha! Ha!

I was back where I belonged. From the Sunnydale Cabaret Lounge to Hollywood and Broadway, via Frinton, and now returning to my first real success, British television. It has been a grand life so far, a Mount Everest of a life – an expedition of highs and even more highs. And I feel sure that I've yet to reach my peak.

So, dear reader, that's really pretty much all I have to say – for now – although there is one adage that everyone in show business agrees is paramount. Always go out with a bang.

So, in conclusion, I have only two words for you.
BOOM! BOOM!

INDEX

☆ ☆ ☆